THE SMARTEST KID
IN THE UNIVERSE

FAVORITES FROM CHRIS GRABENSTEIN

The Island of Dr. Libris
Shine! (coauthored with J.J. Grabenstein)
The Smartest Kid in the Universe

THE MR. LEMONCELLO'S LIBRARY SERIES

Escape from Mr. Lemoncello's Library
Mr. Lemoncello's Library Olympics
Mr. Lemoncello's Great Library Race
Mr. Lemoncello's All-Star Breakout Game
Mr. Lemoncello and the Titanium Ticket

THE WELCOME TO WONDERLAND SERIES

Home Sweet Motel
Beach Party Surf Monkey
Sandapalooza Shake-Up
Beach Battle Blowout

THE HAUNTED MYSTERY SERIES

The Crossroads
The Demons' Door
The Zombie Awakening
The Black Heart Crypt

COAUTHORED WITH JAMES PATTERSON

The House of Robots series
The I Funny series
The Jacky Ha-Ha series
Katt vs. Dogg
The Max Einstein series
Pottymouth and Stoopid
The Treasure Hunters series
Word of Mouse

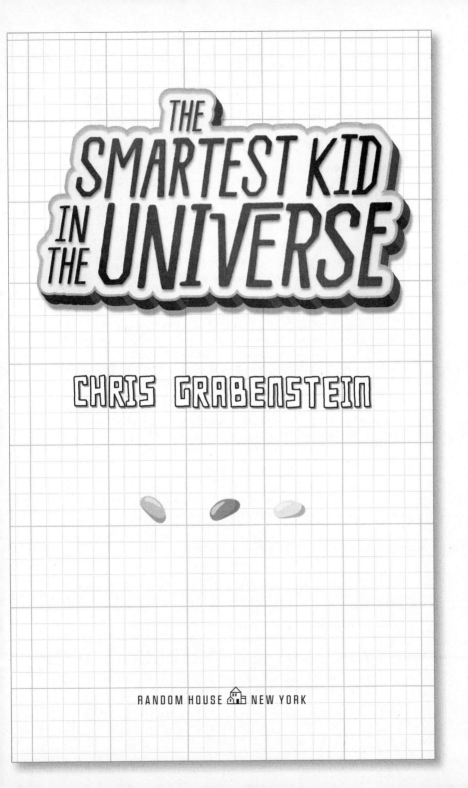

THE SMARTEST KID IN THE UNIVERSE

CHRIS GRABENSTEIN

RANDOM HOUSE 🏠 NEW YORK

Text copyright © 2020 by Chris Grabenstein
Jacket art copyright © 2020 by Antoine Losty
Title lettering copyright © 2020 Neil Swaab

All rights reserved. Published in the United States by Random House Children's Books, a division of Penguin Random House LLC, New York.

Random House and the colophon are registered trademarks of Penguin Random House LLC.

Visit us on the Web! rhcbooks.com

Educators and librarians, for a variety of teaching tools, visit us at
RHTeachersLibrarians.com

Library of Congress Cataloging-in-Publication Data
Names: Grabenstein, Chris, author.
Title: The smartest kid in the universe / Chris Grabenstein.
Description: First edition. | New York: Random House Children's Books, [2020]
Summary: When seventh-grader Jake McQuade mistakes the world's first ingestible knowledge pills for jelly beans, he suddenly knows all about physics and geometry and can speak Swahili (though Spanish would be a lot more useful)—but his sort-of girlfriend Grace thinks they can use his newfound brilliance to save their middle school from the new principal, who is conspiring to get it shut down.
Identifiers: LCCN 2019051235 | ISBN 978-0-525-64778-2 (hardcover) |
ISBN 978-0-525-64779-9 (library binding) | ISBN 978-0-593-30547-8 (int'l) |
ISBN 978-0-525-64780-5 (ebook)
Subjects: LCSH: Genius—Juvenile fiction. | Conspiracies—Juvenile fiction. |
Middle schools—Juvenile fiction. | Humorous stories. | CYAC: Genius—
Fiction. | Conspiracies—Fiction. | Middle schools—Fiction. | Schools—Fiction. |
Humorous stories. | LCGFT: Humorous fiction.
Classification: LCC PZ7.G7487 Sm 2020 | DDC 813.6 [Fic 23]

Printed in Canada
10 9 8 7 6 5 4 3 2 1
First Edition

For Dr. Craig Smith (surgeon), Dr. David Sherman (cardiologist), and all the physicians, physician assistants, nurses, and staff of the Cardiac Care Unit at NewYork-Presbyterian Hospital/Columbia University Medical Center: Thank you all for studying so hard in school.

PROLOGUE

Eduardo Leones wasn't the bravest pirate on Capitán Aliento de Perro's crew.

But he was definitely the smartest.

Because he was the only one not on the sinking ship.

Cannons boomed. Masts snapped. The sky was on fire.

And Eduardo was safe in a bobbing rowboat well below the fray.

"Yarr," cried Aliento de Perro, leaning over the railing and working a line to lower a heavy iron chest. "Row upriver, ye scurvy knave. Find a good hiding place for me booty. Then hurry back to tell me where it be, or you'll end up like your cowardly father!"

"Sí, sí, Capitán," the clever Eduardo shouted back—even though he planned to obey only the first half of that order.

Because the treasure wasn't the captain's.

Aliento de Perro had stolen it from Eduardo's father!

El Perro Apestoso (the *Stinky Dog*), the ship that the blustering pirate Aliento de Perro ("Dog Breath") now commanded, had been seized in an ugly mutiny from Eduardo's father, the brave buccaneer Angel Vengador Leones. After forcing the ship's captain to walk the plank, Aliento de Perro had kept young Eduardo alive only so he could torment the boy.

Now the ship that had plundered and pillaged up and down the east coast of the American colonies was sinking under the relentless attack of a British man-o'-war that had chased it upriver. As a precaution, Dog Breath (who never brushed his teeth) had ordered his cabin boy to haul the ship's treasure to a less treacherous location.

Eduardo grinned as he lashed the heavy chest to the deck of his small vessel.

And then he started rowing. Hard.

North.

The listing pirate ship turned about to block the man-o'-war's pursuit with a broadside of cannon blasts. The British ship roared back with mast-shattering, wood-splintering, sail-searing shots of its own.

The *Stinky Dog* might not be afloat when young Eduardo found a secure spot to hide his captain's treasure.

Which was fine by Eduardo.

He had cleverly tricked Aliento de Perro into thinking

he was too terrified to ever plot revenge. But he *would* avenge his father's death.

All that treasure would become his.

And his children's.

And his children's children's.

And his children's children's children's.

And his children's children's children's children's.

If only they would prove bold and clever enough to find it.

1

Patricia Malvolio, the new principal of Riverview Middle School, was giving a special, after-hours tour of her building to a very important guest: Mr. Heath Huxley.

"This school is in terrible condition!" said Mr. Huxley.

"I know," giggled Mrs. Malvolio. "Isn't it marvelous? It's perfect for our plans."

The lockers were dented and rusty. Overhead, fluorescent lights sputtered in their tubes, pleading to be replaced. Paint peeled off the cinder-block walls in chunks the size of potato chips.

"What's that smell?" asked Mr. Huxley, covering his mouth and nose with a dainty silk handkerchief.

Mrs. Malvolio sniffed the air.

She was tempted to say *Your breath,* since Mr. Huxley's never smelled minty or fresh.

"Tuna fish salad?" she suggested. "Stinky cheese?

Moldy pizza? It's hard to tell. The refrigerators in the cafeteria are . . . unreliable."

Mrs. Malvolio tugged down on the canary-yellow blazer that matched her canary-yellow blouse. The tugging caused her necklace—three rows of big, multicolored beads—to clack.

"Now, as I told you," she said, "Riverview is currently considered the worst middle school building in the district. Given the new budget cuts, the city will be forced to close one middle school this year. I suspect it will be us."

She led the way into her office. Mr. Huxley went to the window to admire the view of the river.

"This is magnificent, Patricia."

"I know. It's why this school is called Riverview."

"And what will the city do with this marvelous property once they shut down this dilapidated excuse for a school?"

"Oh, I suppose they might auction off the land to the highest bidder."

"Who will also be the smartest bidder," said Mr. Huxley, stroking back his slick black hair. "The one who understands how truly valuable this property is."

"Yes, Uncle Heath," said Mrs. Malvolio. "They'll probably sell it to you. And then you'll pay me that very generous finder's fee we discussed when I applied for this principal position."

"Indeed I will, Patricia."

They both laughed maniacally.

It ran in the family.

2

Jake McQuade wasn't the smartest kid at Riverview Middle School, but he was definitely the coolest.

The school itself, on the other hand, was kind of shabby.

The place hadn't fallen apart all at once. If it had, people might've done something. Riverview's decline had been slow and steady. It took time and neglect. No one ever thought to repaint the cinder-block walls. Or to replace the lockers, most of which were too bent out of shape to be locked anymore.

"We try," Mr. Lyons would tell Jake. "We try."

Mr. Charley Lyons was the school's vice principal, a social studies teacher, *and* the basketball coach. He'd been at Riverview for over twenty years.

"But the new principal?" He shook his head. " 'Le zumba el mango,' as my grandfather used to say."

Jake never knew what Mr. Lyons was saying when, all of a sudden, he dropped a little Spanish. Jake would've had to learn Spanish to do that. And seventh grader Jake McQuade wasn't big on "learning stuff." He came to school to have a good time and hang with his friends. If he needed to actually know anything important, he could look it up on his phone.

He stopped by the bathroom to check his look in a mirror. Black hair, blue eyes, and fair, freckled skin. It was a good look. And lately Jake wanted to look good.

Because of Grace.

Grace Garcia!

"How's it going?" Jake said to just about everybody he passed as he cruised up the hall. He was so cool, he could chat with one friend on his cell phone while using his free hand to knock knuckles with a dozen more.

Jake's best friend was Kojo Shelton.

Kojo was a science geek who spent a lot of time streaming detective shows. He called it his extra-credit homework. "Because I'm going to be a detective when I grow up," he'd say, "I need to know forensic science *and* TV detectives."

Recently, Kojo had stumbled upon an ancient show called *Kojak* on some obscure cable rerun channel. He'd become obsessed with the famous TV detective. Kojo even adopted Kojak's famous catchphrase, "Who loves ya, baby?"

"We practically have the same name," he'd told Jake.

"He's Kojak and I'm Kojo. Of course, he's a bald, old Greek dude and I'm a handsome, young Black dude, but, hey—we both like Tootsie Pops."

"I don't," said Jake. "Too much work sucking through that hard candy shell to get to the Tootsie Roll."

"For real? Jake McQuade, you are the laziest kid in the world. You know that, right?"

"We're all good at something, Kojo. Slothfulness? It's my superpower."

Kojo was kind of skinny and always wore the style of thick-rimmed glasses that couldn't get broken when you played sports.

"You wanna go hang in the cafeteria?" asked Jake. "I've got that new *Revenge of the Brain Dead* game on my phone. Mr. Keeney will never miss us."

Mr. Keeney, who taught math, was Jake and Kojo's homeroom teacher. He usually spent the first fifteen minutes of every school day with his feet propped up on his desk, his chair tilted back as far as it could go without tipping over, and his eyes closed.

"This is homeroom," he'd said once. "If I were home, I'd still be sleeping. So keep quiet. I need a nap."

"No thanks, man," Kojo told Jake. "I want to go talk to Mr. Lyons in his office. I need his help on an extra-credit social studies project."

"Is it about the history of this school's vice principal having his office inside an old janitor's closet complete with a mop sink?"

"Nah. Everybody knows the answer to that one: the boy's bathroom on the second floor leaks through the ceiling of the vice principal's office. Has for years. If Mr. Lyons used that office, his hair would be wet. All the time."

"And why are you doing another extra-credit project?"

"Because, Jake, even though I *could* get by on my looks, I prefer to be smart, too. Going for another straight-A report card."

Jake shrugged. "Straight Cs are fine by me."

"You need help on your science homework?"

"Nah. I need to go slay some zombies."

3

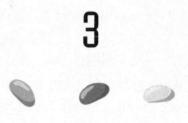

As Jake ambled along the hallway, he saw Grace Garcia hanging a poster on the wall.

Jake wished there were a bathroom mirror nearby. There wasn't.

Grace, another seventh grader, was, without a doubt, the smartest student in the whole school. Jake also thought she was the prettiest. Of course, he'd never tell her that.

"Hey," he said.

"Hey," she said back. Grace was somehow related to Mr. Lyons. Her mom and dad had emigrated from Cuba during the mid-1990s. Mr. Lyons's side of the family had moved to America way earlier, but Grace still called him "Uncle Charley."

"Whatcha doin'?" Jake asked. Yes, he definitely had a way with words when talking to girls.

Grace nodded at the poster. "Trying to find two

new teammates for our Quiz Bowl team. Last year we came in third. This year we're going to win! ¡Comerme un pan!"

Jake nodded. And smiled. And had no idea what *comerme un pan* meant. Judging from the way Grace grinned when she said it, though, it was probably a good thing.

"I lost both my teammates from last year," Grace continued. "One got into Chumley Prep. The other transferred to Sunny Brook."

"Do you have to know facts and stuff to be on the team?" asked Jake.

"Uh, yeah," Grace said with a laugh.

Jake nodded. "Bummer."

A gigantic eighth grader named Noah "No Neck" Nelson strode up the hall. "What's that for?" he said, jabbing a thumb at the poster.

"Our Riverview Pirates Quiz Bowl Team," Grace answered cheerfully. "A friendly but fierce competition against all the other middle schools in our district."

"Quiz Bowl?" snorted Noah. "That's stupid."

He lunged forward to rip the hand-painted poster off the wall, but Jake blocked his move.

"Hey, Noah—speaking of bowls, you ever have one of those taco bowls at Taco Bell?"

"Oh yeah, man. Those are awesome. You can eat the bowl. It's a taco."

"I know. Isn't that amazing?"

"Totally. I like those bread bowls at Panera, too. With the soup inside a scooped-out loaf of bread? I like any bowl you can eat."

"Me too, bro." Jake balled up his fist, Noah balled up his, and they knocked knuckles.

"Catch you later, Jake," said Noah as he strolled away contentedly. "Oh, I almost forgot: you should try the meatball pizza bowl at Olive Garden."

"Thanks for the tip, bro!" Jake called after him.

"No problem, man."

"Thank you," whispered Grace when Noah was gone. "I only made the one poster. Not to be a pesado, but if Noah had ripped it up, I'd be en un lío."

"Yeah," said Jake, even though, once again, he had no idea what Grace meant. "So, uh, Grace—are you trying to teach me Spanish?"

She grinned. "Maybe. Un poco. Don't forget: I saw your report card. You could use a little help in the foreign languages department."

"Hey, I got a C in French. Or, as they say in France, 'un C.'"

Kojo came strutting up the hall. "I love it when a plan comes together," he announced, dropping another catchphrase from another ancient TV show. "Guess what, Grace? Your uncle Charley is going to take me down to the fallout shelter for my extra-credit report."

"Really?" said Grace. "That's sort of off-limits. . . ."

"This school has a fallout shelter?" said Jake.

"Uh-huh," said Kojo. "From the nineteen sixties. You know—the Cuban Missile Crisis. Mr. Lyons's grandfather was the custodian back then and told him all about it. The entrance is in the custodian's closet." Kojo squinted at the Quiz Bowl poster. "You doing that again?"

"Definitely," said Grace.

"Put me down as a maybe," said Kojo. "I have to check my schedule. They're streaming *Columbo* reruns on the Sleuth channel this month."

The bell rang for first period. Well, it kind of clanged like an alarm clock somebody had knocked to the floor one too many times. That meant it was time for homeroom.

"Let me know if you can be on the team, Kojo," said Grace, hurrying off to class. "You'd be awesome!"

"Will do."

Kojo and Jake headed in the opposite direction, to Mr. Keeney's class.

"You really might join the Quiz Bowl team?" asked Jake.

"Sure. If, you know, it doesn't interfere with basketball, my extra-credit social studies project, or my TV shows. When you make it to the top academically, like Grace and I have, Jake, you need to send the elevator back down for the other folks."

"I have no idea what that means, Kojo."

14

"It means if you're smart, you have to help people like you, who, you know, aren't so, uh, academically gifted."

"Gee, thanks, Kojo."

"Hey—who loves ya, baby?"

"Are you going to keep saying that all day?"

"I might, baby. I might."

4

On his way to lunch, Jake saw an extremely lanky kid he didn't recognize.

The guy was holding a slip of paper and turning around in circles.

"You lost?" Jake asked.

"Hardly," the boy replied, looking down at Jake. Jake wasn't offended. He figured the guy was so tall, he looked down on everybody.

"Cool. I'm Jake McQuade."

"Hubert Huxley."

Jake raised a hand to slap a high five. The tall guy left him hanging.

"Can you kindly direct me to Mrs. Malvolio's office?" he asked.

Jake nudged his head to the left. "She's the principal. Her office is *the office*."

"Ah, yes. Smashing."

"Are you British?"

"I beg your pardon?"

"Only British people say 'smashing.' You know, on that TV show. The one where they bake all the cakes."

The kid stared at Jake as if he were an unruly monkey hurling poo at the zoo. "Father was right. This *is* the worst school in the district. Maybe the entire state."

"Whatever. Now, if you'll excuse me, I need to go finish defending Earth from a zombie invasion. Because that's the kind of twenty-first-century skills we're learning here at Riverview Middle School."

Jake hit the cafeteria and quickly completed the next level in *Revenge of the Brain Dead* with one hand while munching on a cheeseburger with the other.

"Book 'em, Jake-o!" said Kojo, peering over Jake's shoulder. "That's from *Hawaii Five-O,* only the dude's name is Danno, not Jake-o."

"You ever think you watch too much TV?" asked Jake.

"No such thing, baby."

Mrs. Malvolio marched into the lunchroom. She was carrying a thick stack of papers. Hubert Huxley, the tall kid Jake had met earlier, was walking behind her. They made a beeline for Grace Garcia's table.

"Miss Garcia?" the principal said with a smile.

"Yes, Mrs. Malvolio?"

"This is Hubert Huxley. He goes to Sunny Brook Middle School."

"Top middle school in the district," said Hubert, bouncing proudly on his heels. "I'm the student council president and, of course, captain of the basketball team."

Mrs. Malvolio waved her stack of papers in the air. "I have completed the paperwork you'll need," she said to Grace.

"Um, to do what?"

Mrs. Malvolio smiled. "To transfer to Sunny Brook."

"We're putting together our Quiz Bowl team," said Hubert. "You were pretty good in last year's competition, even though your teammates stank. We'd love to have you try out for our squad. You'd have a much better chance of winning at Sunny Brook."

"I've seen your file, Miss Garcia," said the principal. "You earn straight As. You excel on all the state tests. You deserve better than we can currently offer you here at Riverview. You deserve to be at Sunny Brook."

Grace smiled. "Mrs. Malvolio?"

"Yes, dear?"

"I appreciate the offer."

"Good!"

"But I want to stay here with my uncle Charley."

"Who's he?" scoffed Hubert.

"My so-called vice principal," muttered Mrs. Malvolio with a dismissive roll of her eyes. "Someone from Miss Garcia's family has been on staff here ever since Riverview opened."

"That's the weirdest reason for staying at a school that I've ever heard," said Hubert.

Grace grinned mysteriously. "Well, you don't know my family. We're tight. Always have been. Always will be."

5

After school, Jake and Kojo suited up with the rest of the Riverview Pirates for a basketball game against the Sunny Brook Cougars.

"Is that what you're wearing?" Kojo said when he saw Jake's baggy shorts. Actually, they were sweatpants with the legs cut off at the knees. Jake was also wearing a T-shirt that read, MATH: THE ONLY PLACE WHERE PEOPLE CAN BUY 87 WATERMELONS AND NOBODY WONDERS WHY.

"Yeah," said Jake with a shrug. "Everything else is in my dirty-clothes bag."

"Your mother ever teach you how to do laundry?"

"She's tried. I'm a slow learner. Especially when it comes to household chores. I can almost set the table. *Almost.*"

Kojo shook his head and put on his official black-and-gold Pirates uniform.

"Jake?" said Mr. Lyons in his after-school role as the basketball coach. "Why can't you remember to bring your uniform on game days?"

"Because it's hard?" offered Jake.

"Hard? How hard can it be? 'I have a basketball game today. I should bring my basketball uniform to school.' What's hard about that?"

"Well, sir, first you need a calendar, to know what day it is. And then you have to remember to write down all the games in the little boxes on that calendar. Then you have to remember to *look* at that calendar on game days. That's a lotta work, sir. A lotta, lotta work."

Mr. Lyons closed his eyes and mumbled something to himself. It could've been *Why do I even bother?* Jake wasn't sure.

"Okay, guys," Mr. Lyons said right before it was time to leave the locker room and hit the floor. "Sunny Brook is tough. Their center is a six-foot giant named Hubert Huxley. The boy is humongous. But I outlined a play that I think will allow us to get into the paint and score on their big man. . . ."

He drew a play with a marker on a whiteboard. There were a lot of circles and arrows. Some dots and dashes, too. Jake had no idea what any of it meant. He figured he'd just run the play he always ran: Toss the ball around. Take random shots. See if anybody could hit the basket. Or the backboard. Odds were something would eventually bounce the right way and drop through the hoop.

That was not what happened.

Riverview lost to Sunny Brook, 120–12. (Kojo scored six times.) After the game, Mr. Lyons called a team meeting in the locker room.

"Winning isn't everything," he said. "But you guys aren't even trying. You aren't playing up to your potential."

"Yes, we are," said Jake. "We lost. It's what we do best."

Mr. Lyons sighed one of his deep sighs and walked away.

"I wouldn't mind winning," Kojo muttered after Mr. Lyons was gone.

"Nah," said Jake. "We're better off losing. There's a ton less stress."

"Well," said Kojo, "we're just gonna have to agree to disagree."

And for the first time in a long time, Kojo didn't want to walk home with Jake.

6

On Thursday night, Jake and his little sister, Emma, were home alone.

Their mom was busy at her high-stress job as an events coordinator at the Imperial Marquis, a big downtown hotel. Ms. Michelle McQuade was excellent at her job. Super responsible, organized, and efficient.

She was the exact opposite of her son.

Emma, a fourth grader, was three years younger than Jake. Technically, he was her big brother, even though he wasn't very good with much of the typical big-brother stuff—like helping her do homework.

"I need help," said Emma, even though she wished she didn't have to say it. "With math, not Spanish."

Emma went to a Spanish-immersion elementary school. She knew Jake would be useless helping her with her bilingual language skills. But she figured he would at least know how to solve a fourth-grade math problem.

They were sitting in the kitchen. Emma was working on her homework. Jake was working on his phone, slicing watermelons in a game app called *Fruit Ninja*.

"Hang on. Goin' for a five-fruit combo slice." Jake swiped his finger across the screen of his phone. "Ah, missed." He put down his device and gave Emma a *gimme-gimme* hand gesture. "What's the problem?"

Emma read off her worksheet. " 'At Billy's Bakery, cupcakes cost fifty-three cents.' "

Jake nodded. "Decent price. Go on."

" 'Bagels cost a dollar twenty-five.' "

"Plain? Or with butter?"

"I don't know."

"What about cream cheese?"

"There's no cream cheese in the math problem, Jake."

"There should be. Or butter. Who wants to eat a dry bagel?"

Emma rolled her eyes and read the last sentence in the word problem. " 'How much more do two bagels cost than two cupcakes?' "

Jake stroked his chin and pondered the question. "Do the cupcakes have frosting?"

Emma shrugged. "I guess."

"Okay. Here's your answer: too much!"

"Huh?"

"The two bagels cost way too much compared to the two cupcakes. The bagels are incomplete. No butter? No cream cheese? Not even margarine? The cupcakes, on the other hand, are fully frosted. Therefore, two bagels cost way too much compared to two cupcakes." He pointed at the answer line on Emma's worksheet. "Write down 'Way too much.'"

"That's not the right answer. Mrs. Valiente is going to give me an F!"

"Billy is ripping off his customers, Emma. Instead of writing math problems about the guy, they should arrest him!"

Jake's phone vibrated and sounded its text alert: a funny armpit-fart ringtone.

"It's Mom," said Jake, glancing at the screen. "She has to work late. Big event. Says we need to fix our own dinner." Jake looked around the kitchen. "Is there any money left in the pizza jar?"

Emma shook her head. "We used it up the last time Mom had to work late. Last night."

"Come on," said Jake, standing up. "You have your bus pass?"

"Um, yeah. But why do I need it? There's microwavable dinners in the freezer."

"Too much work," said Jake. "If Mom has a big event

25

down at the hotel, that means there's a ton of food. Your choice of chicken, beef, or fish."

"I prefer the vegetarian option."

"Fine. You can have the pasta with peas and cauliflower. We're taking a bus downtown. It's suppertime!"

7

Jake and Emma caught an express bus downtown.

Fifteen minutes later, stomachs grumbling, they hopped off and bustled up the alley that would take them to the service entrance behind the Imperial Marquis Hotel. The building was forty stories tall. Its ballroom could seat five hundred banquet guests at once. The kitchen that turned out all that food was ginormous.

Jake and Emma's mom was in charge of making sure big banquets in the Imperial Marquis's convention and meeting facilities went off without a hitch.

"What's up, you guys?" said Tony, one of the hotel's event staff. He was hanging out on the loading dock while everybody else hustled their butts off.

"Shouldn't you be inside, helping out?" said Emma.

"I'm on my break."

"In the middle of a banquet?"

Tony shrugged. "I don't make the schedule."

"What's the big event?" asked Jake.

"Some dude named Dr. Sinclair Blackbridge is giving a talk to a bunch of brainiacs," said Tony. "Blackbridge is a futurist. From MIT."

"The Massachusetts Institute of Technology?" said Emma, sounding impressed.

"I guess," said Tony with another shrug.

"What's a futurist?" asked Jake.

"A fancy fortune-teller with a bunch of college degrees. He uses science and computers to predict the future. He can tell you what's going to happen in ten, twenty years."

"He any good?" asked Jake.

"Seems like it. I mean, he can't tell you who's going to win tonight's game or nothin', but way back in 1995, he predicted that we'd use computers to buy junk on the internet. Everybody laughed at him. Turns out he was right. Turns out he's always right. He predicted GPS navigation devices for cars before anybody else, too. And those E-ZPass things on the turnpike so you don't have to slow down or stop to pay tolls. The guy's legit. A real scientific soothsayer."

"So, what's for dinner?"

"Chicken, fish, or beef."

"Is there a vegetarian option?" asked Emma.

"Cheese ravioli. Go grab something. We always make extra."

"And we always appreciate it," said Jake. He knocked knuckles with Tony. He and Emma headed into the kitchen.

"Hey, Jake," said a server, a guy named Arturo. "Hola, Emma."

"Hola, Arturo," said Emma. "¿Cómo estás?"

"Bien, ¿y tú?"

"Muy bien, gracias."

Arturo was one of their mother's hardest workers. He was toting a tray loaded down with at least a dozen domed plates. "You kids hungry?" he asked.

"Does it show?" joked Jake.

"We're right in the middle of serving the main course. Go grab a seat in the greenroom. The speaker's done using it. I'll hook you guys up in about fifteen. Cool?"

"Cool," said Jake.

"You want the ravioli, Emma?"

"Sí. Muchas gracias, Arturo."

"No problem. Just hang and chill. We've got that chocolate mousse cake with the raspberries on top for dessert, too."

"Definitely worth the wait," said Jake. "Thanks, man."

He led the way into what everybody called the greenroom: a small cinder-block cubbyhole with a couch, a table, a couple of chairs, and a private bathroom. It was a place where guest speakers could wait or rehearse before they went into the banquet hall to give their talks.

There was also a video monitor where you could watch and listen to what was going on in the dining room. Right now it was mostly hubbub, laughter, and the sound of clinking plates and tumbling ice as uniformed servers whisked around the room with their heavy trays and pitchers of water. Somewhere, probably in the shadows, Jake and Emma's mom was orchestrating all the action over her headset.

"I'm starving," Jake grumbled, twisting the volume knob next to the video monitor to mute the sound. "Watching all those people chowing down in there makes it worse."

"If you were that hungry," said Emma, "we should've just nuked a frozen cheeseburger back home."

"This is easier," said Jake.

Emma shook her head and went into the bathroom.

Jake spied a glass jar of jelly beans sitting on the green-room table.

It was a small jar with a wire-clasped lid. There were only about two or three dozen brightly colored jelly beans sealed inside. A small snack. Just enough for one hungry kid.

Just enough for Jake.

So, since Emma was out of the room, and since nobody had labeled the jar as theirs, Jake popped open the top and gobbled down the jelly beans, one fistful at a time.

They were pretty tasty. Not as good as Jelly Bellys, but definitely Easter basket–quality stuff.

By the time Emma came back into the room, the jelly beans were gone.

And even though he didn't know it yet, Jake McQuade's life was never, ever going to be the same.

8

Dr. Sinclair Blackbridge spoke after the dinner and dessert dishes had been cleared, after Jake and Emma had finished their delicious meals and headed for home on the uptown bus (without their mother knowing they'd even been at the Imperial Marquis for dinner).

As Dr. Blackbridge left the stage, he was mobbed by a crowd of eager admirers, all of whom wanted to shake his hand, congratulate him on his genius, have him sign a book, or ask a follow-up question.

One of those admirers was an intense young scientist and inventor named Haazim Farooqi, who had come to America from Pakistan to study biochemistry. Farooqi was only thirty-three years old, but he was a genius, even if nobody (other than his mother) knew it.

"Professor Blackbridge?" he cried out. "Professor Blackbridge?"

The MIT scholar pretended he couldn't hear Farooqi.

"I know you can hear me, sir," shouted Farooqi. "I'm speaking very loudly, and you're only three feet away. The elementary physics of sound waves assures me that you are receiving my auditory signals."

"How did you even get in here tonight, Haazim?" said Blackbridge as he scribbled an autograph in a book a fan had thrust at him.

"Well, sir," said Farooqi, "I'm rather determined."

"And I'm rather busy."

"But, Dr. Blackbridge, sir, I've had a breakthrough! I think. I mean, I won't know for sure until we run a series of rigorous tests."

He finally had Blackbridge's attention. *"We?"*

Farooqi beamed. "Yes, sir. You and me. Together we'll make your most recent prediction come true."

Blackbridge chuckled and shifted his focus to signing another copy of his book. "I'm a thinker, not a doer, young man," he said without bothering to look at Farooqi.

The young biochemist wasn't discouraged. "That's why you need me, sir. I'm a doer. In fact, I already did it. It's done. I left it for you. It's backstage. In the greenroom, sir."

"I'm not returning to the greenroom. My driver is waiting out front. I need to be at the airport."

"But—"

"Call my assistant. We might be able to find some time for you on my calendar."

"No, sir. I already called. Your assistant told me you're completely booked. For the next ten years. Wait. Don't leave. I'll go grab my prototypes. You can take them with you. Maybe do your own research."

"My car is waiting. . . ."

"I know. I'll be quick, sir. Trust me—you don't want to leave this hotel without proof that what you just predicted can actually come true. Not in thirty years. Not in twenty. But tomorrow. Today!"

A fresh wave of well-wishers and glad-handers swamped Professor Blackbridge, pushing Farooqi farther and farther away. One of Blackbridge's handlers was attempting to guide the esteemed theoretical thinker toward the exit.

Farooqi didn't have much time.

He raced out of the ballroom and entered the kitchen.

He dashed into the greenroom to grab his container of samples.

He froze in horror.

His jar of jelly beans was empty.

His precious, one-of-a-kind, irreplaceable prototypes were gone!

9

Jake and Emma, their bellies full, rumbled back uptown on a city bus.

This one was a local, making all the stops.

Emma carried a white paper shopping bag filled with "leftovers" from their backstage banquet feast: an aluminum tray of cheese ravioli and two extra slices of chocolate mousse cake with raspberries on top.

"Emma, did you know that chocolate was introduced to France by the Spanish in the seventeenth century?" said Jake.

Emma shook her head.

"Chocolate mousse, which of course means 'foam' and not an antlered cousin of elk, has been a staple of French cuisine since the eighteenth century."

Now Emma was staring at Jake.

"Raspberries, on the other hand, are believed to have

originated in Greece. The scientific name for red raspberries is *Rubus idaeus*. That means 'bramblebush of Ida,' named for the mountain where they grew on the island of Crete."

"What are you talking about?" said Emma. "How do you know all this stuff?"

Jake shrugged. *How do I know this stuff?*

"Beats me."

The bus lurched to another air brake–hissing stop.

A family—a mom, a dad, and two kids—seated directly across from Jake and Emma near the back of the bus looked at a map and then at each other nervously.

"Hiki ndicho kikomo chetu?" said the mom.

"Sina uhakika," said the dad, sounding anxious.

Jake smiled. "Unataka kwenda wapi?" he asked.

"You speak Swahili?" asked the somewhat surprised father.

"Of course he doesn't," said Emma.

"Ndiyo," replied Jake. "Ndiyo, nadhani nafanya."

The father, speaking Swahili, told Jake that their hotel was located on West Fifty-Ninth Street.

"Ah," Jake replied, also in Swahili, "then you will need to exit the bus in two more stops."

"Thank you, young man!" said the mother.

"Thank you," said the two children. All of them were still speaking Swahili, and so was Jake.

"Karibu," he said. "Furahia jioni yako yote."

"What'd you just tell those people?" asked Emma.

"I said, 'You're welcome. Enjoy the rest of your evening.'"

"You speak Swahili?"

"I guess. I mean, I think I just did."

"You can't help me with my Spanish homework, but you speak Swahili?"

"It's just something I picked up," Jake said nervously. "And not from Kojo. His grandfather came to America from Zimbabwe, a landlocked country in southern Africa that's bordered by South Africa, Botswana, Zambia, and Mozambique."

Emma was gawking at her big brother as if he were a freak. Jake couldn't blame her. The words tumbling out of his mouth were kind of freakish.

"In Zimbabwe," he continued, "there are sixteen official languages, none of which is Swahili. Those official languages are Chewa, Chibarwe, English—"

Emma cut him off. "And how'd you know all that stuff about chocolate mousse and raspberries?"

"I don't know," Jake replied. His palms were starting to sweat. His stomach felt queasy, too.

HOW DO I KNOW THIS STUFF?

"Are you feeling okay, Jake?" whispered Emma, sounding seriously worried.

"Not really."

"You're sweating."

"Yeah," said Jake. "I guess I shouldn't've eaten the beef *and* the chicken."

"You wolfed down two slices of cake, too. With extra chocolate sauce."

Jake nodded. "I think I gave myself indigestion."

"And that makes you know Swahili, African geography, and the history of food?" said Emma. "Usually it just makes me burp."

"I need to go home and go to bed."

"We should call Mom. You might need to see a doctor."

"No. It's just indigestion. Of course, indigestion, also known as dyspepsia, is a term that describes a wide range of gastrointestinal maladies."

"Jake?"

"Yeah, Emma?"

"You're scaring me."

"I know. I'm scaring me, too!"

10

The next morning, Jake realized he probably should tell his mom about the weird stuff that started happening when he and Emma left the hotel.

But then he'd have to tell her he'd disobeyed her orders (again) and dragged Emma down to the Imperial Marquis (again) to mooch a free gourmet meal off the hotel staff (again).

So instead he sat quietly at the breakfast table and ate his cereal. When Emma gave him a worried look, Jake shifted his focus to the back of the cereal box and read about how Cheerios were "oatstanding," and somehow he knew that Cheerios were originally called Cherrioats back in 1941, but the name was changed in 1945.

"What'd you guys do for dinner last night?" Mom asked, guzzling coffee.

"Nothing," said Jake, because that was his go-to answer for all sorts of Mom questions.

"Seriously?" she said, raising her eyebrows. "You didn't feed your little sister?"

"We nuked a couple of frozen burritos," said Jake. "Of course, the precise origin of burritos isn't known. According to Wikipedia, some speculate that they might have originated in the eighteen hundreds among the vaqueros, the cowboys of northern Mexico."

Now Jake's mother was staring at him, too.

"The ones in our refrigerator came from the grocery store," she said. "They originated in the freezer section."

"Riiight. Good to know. Well, I gotta run."

"Say hi to Kojo for me," said his mom. "Is he still fixated on that old TV show *Kojak*?"

Jake just nodded. He was afraid that if he said everything he somehow suddenly knew about *Kojak*—that the show aired on CBS from 1973 to 1978, with Telly Savalas starring as Theo Kojak, an NYPD detective whose catchphrase was "Who loves ya, baby?"—she'd want to take his temperature and then drag him off to see a doctor. Maybe a child psychiatrist. Not that the psychiatrist would be a child. After all, it takes eight years of post-undergraduate study to become board certified. . . .

Jake forced himself to stop thinking.

He did okay until third period, when Mr. Lyons passed out a social studies pop quiz.

Everybody (except Kojo) groaned. But not Jake. He knew that the first permanent French colony in the New World had been Quebec, that the Philippines were named after King Philip II of Spain, and that Jacques Cartier had discovered the St. Lawrence River.

Jake knew everything. The answers to all twenty questions.

He completed the pop quiz in record time (ninety-three seconds) and was impressed by his much-improved handwriting. It looked like something you'd see on a really cool chalkboard at a coffee shop.

Mr. Lyons saw Jake just sitting there with his quiz sheet turned over on his desk. "Aren't you even going to try, Jake?"

"I already finished, sir."

Mr. Lyons sighed and held out his hand. "Let me see what you came up with this time."

Jake turned in his test. Mr. Lyons scanned it quickly. Then he studied it more slowly. Then he smiled.

"Well done, Mr. McQuade. What did you eat for breakfast this morning?"

"Cheerios, sir. Which, by the way, used to be called Cheerioats between 1941 and 1945."

"Is that so? Fascinating. Did you, by any chance, remember to bring your basketball uniform to school today?"

"Yes, sir. It's in my locker."

And Mr. Lyons's smile grew even wider.

* * *

"Way to go, baby," said Kojo when he saw that Jake had aced the pop quiz. "You got a hundred, just like me. I'm glad I could be such an inspiration to you."

That afternoon, thanks to Mr. Lyons's play diagrams and Jake's practical application of geometry and trigonometry in the execution of those plays, coupled with his on-the-fly mathematical calculations of shot probability and a laser-sharp focus on the parabola, or curve, of all his shots—not to mention feeding the ball to Kojo at precisely the right instant so he could also score—the Riverview Pirates won their first game in five years.

All in all, it had been a pretty good day.

And Jake McQuade had no idea how he'd done any of it.

11

That night, Jake, Emma, and their mom sat down to dinner.

It was takeout from a local chicken place; Mom had grabbed the food on her way home from work.

"No events in the ballroom tonight," she said, brushing back her hair. "Thank goodness. Dig in, guys. I got fried chicken for you, Jake. Salad for Emma. Rotisserie chicken for me. And mashed potatoes for everybody!"

Jake's mom was in her early forties and very pretty. A lot of guys wanted to ask her out on dates. But she wasn't interested. "One husband was enough for me," she'd say with a laugh.

Like always, Jake used the bottom of his spoon to form a crater in his mashed potatoes. One that was deep enough to hold a pool of gravy. All of a sudden, it reminded him of the crater lake in the Philippines called

Pinatubo, which was created after the 1991 eruption of the Mount Pinatubo volcano.

Why do I know that?

And why do I know that the Philippines is an archipelagic country consisting of 7,641 islands?

How do I even know the word archipelagic?

Suddenly he realized something: all this started happening *after* they had left the hotel. *Did the ballroom speaker, the futurist guy, have something to do with what's going on?*

"So, Mom," he said, trying his best to make sure his voice didn't squeak, "exactly who was speaking at the hotel last night?"

"Dr. Sinclair Blackbridge," she replied. "The place was packed. He's a very famous technology prophet. His TED Talk, 'Our Brilliant Tomorrow,' has been watched nearly two million times online."

"Dr. Blackbridge talked with some guy named Ted?" asked Emma.

Mom laughed a little. "No, Emma. 'T-E-D' stands for 'Technology, Entertainment, and Design.' Speakers at TED conferences give short, powerful talks. It's all about spreading ideas."

"And what idea was Dr. Blackbridge spreading last night?" asked Jake.

"He more or less repeated his TED Talk and predicted that the future, the world you two will live in, will be a very smart place."

Jake nodded. It seemed like Dr. Blackbridge's prediction might've come true. At least for Jake.

Dinner done and dishes cleaned, Emma and Jake went to their rooms to finish their homework. Actually, Jake had finished his in ten minutes after he got home, which was another major surprise. He usually didn't bother with homework. He agreed with all those who said middle schoolers need extra sleep to grow and develop. He believed they also need extra video games. And extra time for texting.

But that night—in addition to the math, science, social studies, and ELA assignments he'd already nailed—he was going to do some research. He was going to watch Dr. Sinclair Blackbridge's famous TED Talk.

He hoped it might offer some clue as to what the heck had happened to him at the Imperial Marquis Hotel.

12

Jake went to the TED website.

A quick search took him to Dr. Blackbridge's famous lecture. He clicked play, and the video started streaming. Soon a very distinguished, silver-haired man in an open-collar white shirt and black suit strode onto a stage. He was wearing a microphone looped over his ear. The audience applauded eagerly.

After the ovation ended, Dr. Blackbridge went down the list of things he had successfully predicted in the past. Smartphones. Touch-screen computer control. GPS navigational devices in cars. Computers in classrooms. Intercontinental video calls over the internet. Toll gates where you didn't have to stop to pay.

"So, what is my next prediction?" he asked his audience with a sly twinkle in his eye. "Well, it's just that. A prediction. I'm nearly eighty years old, so I won't be around to see it, because I am convinced it will take thirty, maybe forty, years before someone figures out precisely how to do it. But, my friends, the future will be all about IK. It will revolutionize everything. And what, you might wonder, is IK? Simple: Ingestible Knowledge."

The crowd gasped. Jake did, too.

"For centuries, we humans have consumed information through our eyes and our ears. By reading. Or listening to lectures like this one. We can also learn a lot through our senses of smell and touch—like why one should avoid boiled cabbage or climbing thorny rosebushes."

His audience chuckled.

"But our senses may not be the most efficient channel for learning. So here is my prediction: In the not-too-distant future, we are going to ingest information. You're going to swallow a pill and know English. You're going to swallow a pill and know geometry, trigonometry, and quantum physics. You'll take another pill and instantly speak Swahili."

Jake's jaw nearly fell to his sneakers when Dr. Black-bridge said that.

"This will all happen," the professor continued, "through the bloodstream. Molecules of knowledge will float up to your brain and deposit themselves in all the right cells and synapses. You won't need to read a book or attend lectures to understand Shakespeare. The chemicals in these pills will do your learning for you."

The crowd in the TED Talk audience looked stunned. Dr. Blackbridge smiled when he saw their reaction.

"I suppose these smart pills might put a few of our top colleges and universities out of business."

A nervous titter ran through the crowd.

"But don't panic, fellow professors. We're talking about the future. Ingestible Knowledge can't be done. Not yet, anyhow. You still have thirty or forty years of job security."

Jake's fingers were trembling when he tapped the screen to end the video.

Had he somehow accidentally ingested knowledge last night at the hotel?

Impossible. He'd had the chicken and the beef and a couple slices of cake. None of those were pills.

Besides, Emma had eaten the cake, too, and she hadn't become an instant genius.

That was when he remembered the jelly beans.

13

"Jelly beans?" said Kojo. "You aced that social studies quiz and made all those shots in the basketball game because you ate jelly beans?"

Jake nodded. "I think so."

"You have any more?" Kojo asked. "Because I'd like to sink buckets the way you did. Tell me again how you did it? Is it like carbo-loading before a marathon?"

"No. I used geometry and focused on the parabola of my shots. I also knew exactly when to feed you the ball, based on timing and patterns I was seeing on the floor."

"Uh-huh."

Jake kept going. "A parabola, as you probably know, is the arched trajectory naturally formed by any projectile— a missile, a rotten tomato, or a basketball—moving in a gravitational field. The higher the parabola, the more easily the ball drops through the hoop. The lower, the greater the probability that the ball will hit the rim. That's why you need to follow through with your wrist, give the ball a quick little backflip at the end of the shot."

"For the parabola?"

"Correct."

"Okay," said Kojo. "We need to head to your mom's hotel. See if there are any more magical jelly beans lying around. I want to get my parabola on, too."

Right after the final bell, Jake and Kojo caught an express bus downtown. They made their way up the alley to the hotel's service entrance. Like always, Tony was on the loading dock, taking a break.

"Hey, Jake. How's it going?"

"Fine, I guess. This is my best friend, Kojo."

"Nice to meet you, Kojo."

Kojo shook Tony's hand. "Who loves ya, baby?"

Tony shrugged. "I dunno. My mother? So, Jake, you guys looking for *your* mother? She's probably up front in her office."

Jake shook his head.

"We're here for the jelly beans," blurted Kojo.

"The jelly beans?" said Tony, sounding confused.

"Two nights ago," Jake explained, "Emma and I were hanging out in the greenroom. There was this jar of jelly beans."

Tony slapped himself in the forehead. "Oh. Right. The jelly beans. I forgot to put the goofy little guy's business card on the table with them."

"Huh?" said Jake.

"That was the night this wild-eyed mad-scientist dude came by. I could tell he was a brainiac. One of those absentminded-professor types, you know what I mean?"

Jake and Kojo nodded.

"Anyway, he *really* wanted to leave Professor Black-bridge a present in the greenroom, even though Black-bridge had already gone into the banquet hall to eat dinner with his fans. The young guy had a jar full of jelly beans. I pointed to the sign: 'Authorized Personnel Only.' He can't go backstage. All of a sudden, he's peeling off twenty-dollar bills. Says he'll give me a hundred bucks if I put his gift in the greenroom. So I did. Only I forgot to tuck his business card under the jar like I was supposed to. Oops."

Tony dug out his wallet and pulled a smudged and crinkled business card from its billfold.

" 'Haazim Farooqi,' " he read off the card. "Later the guy comes running up to me, claiming somebody stole his jelly beans. I told him I don't like jelly beans. I'm more of a Reese's Peanut Butter Cup–type guy. Anyway, Farooqi's going nuts. Screaming at me. Whining about his jelly beans. Saying they were supposed to go to Dr. Black-bridge. Finally, I had to call Omar from security to come haul the kook out of here."

"Does his business card have an address on it?" Jake asked.

Tony glanced at the card.

"Yeah."

"Can I have it?"

"What for?"

"Well, uh, Kojo and I are working on a project. For school."

"That's right," said Kojo. "It's all about jelly beans and parabolas."

"Huh?"

"Did you know," said Jake, "that jelly beans were first mentioned in 1861 when a Boston confectioner named William Schrafft urged people to send his small bean-shaped candies to soldiers during the American Civil War? Then, in 1963, fans of the Beatles—"

"Here!" said Tony, terrified that Jake could go on for hours about jelly beans (he could). "Take the guy's card. Just don't bore me to death with more jelly bean trivia."

"Thanks, Tony."

Jake took the card and studied what was printed on it:

HAAZIM FAROOQI
Inventor of First-Generation IK

Room C-13, Corey Hall, Warwick College

www.beans4brains.net

Kojo peered over Jake's shoulder. "What's 'IK'?"

Jake swallowed hard before he answered. "Ingestible Knowledge."

14

Jake used his phone to check out Haazim Farooqi's website, beans4brains.net.

It had one of those yellow-and-black banners saying it was under construction.

"Guess it's a startup that hasn't exactly started up," said Kojo.

"We should go visit him."

"Good idea. But how do we get there?"

"Simple. We take the downtown nine bus, transfer at Tenth Street for the crosstown twelve, take that to Arlington Avenue, where we can hop on the number fifteen, which will take us the remaining eight blocks to Warwick College. Given current traffic conditions, I estimate total transit time to be approximately twenty-nine minutes, plus or minus ten minutes, depending on how speedily we are able to transfer between buses."

Kojo nodded. "One of those jelly beans linked to a travel app?"

"I guess."

"Cool. Let's boogie, baby."

"That's not Kojak's catchphrase."

"I know. But it's going to be one of mine!"

Jake and Kojo boarded the first bus, where Jake helped a kid coming home from school conjugate a Latin verb.

"To love. Amo, amas, amat, amamus, amatis, amant!"

On the crosstown bus, he taught a second grader how to memorize the order of the planets in the solar system. "My Very Easy Method Just Speeds Up Naming Planets."

"Okay," said the boy. "What is it?"

"That sentence. M-V-E-M-J-S-U-N-P. Mercury, Venus, Earth, Mars, Jupiter, Saturn, Uranus, Neptune, and Pluto."

"Technically, Pluto's not a planet anymore," Kojo told the second grader. "But it is still considered a *dwarf planet*."

"So, so true," said Jake.

Kojo shook his head like he was trying to clear it. "This is weird, bro. You knowing stuff like me."

"I know!"

The bus ride down Arlington Avenue was extremely short, so Jake amused himself by silently factoring percentages for passengers versus bus capacity and average number of potholes per city block.

* * *

They hopped off the bus, saw the big arched entryway for Warwick College, and made their way onto the campus. A winding path led them past stately buildings with Greek columns and across a grassy space known as the Willoughby Quad because, as Jake informed Kojo, "it was named after Willoughby Wanamaker Warwick, the popular founder and first dean of Warwick College."

"TMI, bro," said Kojo. "TMI. Let's just find Corey Hall."

They finally did. It took some doing. But after a series of switchbacks, twists, and turns, they stood in front of a three-story redbrick building, tucked behind the Science and Engineering Library. Most of the windows in Corey Hall were dark. There were also signs of construction— a barrel-shaped cement mixer and a dumpster filled with debris. A posted sign read, PARDON OUR DUST, BUT REMODEL WE MUST.

"The place looks deserted," said Jake.

"Except for that security guard in the lobby," said Kojo. "Let me handle this. On TV, detectives and spies are always looking for people, getting in where folks don't want them to get in. I've been studying their moves."

"Great," said Jake. "Thanks."

Kojo unwrapped a Tootsie Pop and tucked it into his mouth. He hiked up his pants, smoothed out his shirt, and strode into the lobby.

"Good afternoon, ma'am," he said to the security guard stationed near the entrance. "This will only take a minute. We're looking for Haazim Farooqi. Name ring a bell?"

"Downstairs," said the lady.

"Excuse me?"

"He's downstairs. Subbasement C. Take the elevator on the left. It's the only one that goes down that far."

"Thanks for the four-one-one, ma'am. Come on, Jake. You heard the lady. We need to be downstairs."

Kojo jabbed the nubby down button for the elevator. There was a *thunk*, a *whirr*, and the sound of grinding gears as the elevator car slowly creaked its way through the shaft. Finally the door slid open, and the two friends stepped aboard.

Jake pressed C. Several times.

When the door rattled shut (with an assist from Kojo), the elevator shuddered and started its very slow descent.

"You think they have gerbils on exercise wheels powering this thing?" joked Kojo.

"No. I suspect they're utilizing pulleys, cables, and counterweights, as is customary."

"Riiiight."

When they reached the subbasement, the elevator door skidded sideways, opening up on a dimly lit hallway where the ceiling was filled with a jumble of hanging pipes and dusty ductwork. A bulletin board on the far cinderblock wall displayed one faded flyer. For something that happened ten years earlier.

"Guess nobody comes down here much," said Kojo.

"Guess not."

They crept along the empty corridor. Somewhere a furnace thrummed. Steam hissed through pipes overhead.

"Here we go." Jake nodded toward a battleship-gray steel door. "Room C-Thirteen."

"Stand back. I'll handle this." Kojo banged his balled-up fist against the door. "Yo. Mr. Haazim Farooqi, if that's really your name. Open up. Official business."

"Maybe you shouldn't knock so loudly," suggested Jake.

"What? Have you been studying TV detective shows like I have? Or did one of those jelly beans you wolfed down—"

The door swung open to reveal a wide-eyed young man in a white lab coat, rumpled white shirt, crooked bow tie, plaid shorts, knee-high socks, and sandals. His dark hair was sticking out in wild spikes, as if he'd been tugging on it all day. He had stubble on his chin and bags underneath his bulging eyes.

"Jelly beans?" he said hastily. "What do you two know about jelly beans?"

15

Farooqi looked up and down the hall like a nervous ferret, then dragged Jake and Kojo into his room.

C-13 appeared to be some sort of chemistry lab. There were beakers and bottles and test tubes everywhere. A Bunsen burner's hissing blue flame was making a round-bottomed bottle full of purple goop burble and bubble. Stacks of paper and empty takeout cartons were piled on a pair of antique metal desks. A bulky computer—one that looked like it was born in the late 1990s—randomly blinked on a rack. Several pairs of argyle socks were draped over one of the exposed pipes hanging from the ceiling. There was a dead plant in the open top drawer of a dented filing cabinet.

Haazim Farooqi's IK lab was definitely low-tech and old-school.

"I'll ask again," said the frazzled scientist. "What do

you two know about my jelly beans?" There was panic in his eyes.

Jake explained everything as quickly as he could.

How Tony had put the jelly beans in the greenroom, backstage at the hotel. How Jake had seen them and, since they weren't labeled or marked in any way, gobbled them down.

"When we went back to the hotel," Jake explained, "Tony gave us your business card. The one he was supposed to put with the jelly beans for Dr. Blackbridge. I know about IK. I know because I think I ingested a whole bunch of knowledge when I ingested those jelly beans."

Farooqi's eyes brightened as they darted back and forth.

"Did anybody follow you here?"

"No," said Kojo. "I know how to lose a tail."

Farooqi glared at him. "Did you eat some of my jelly beans, too?"

"No, man. I just watch a lot of TV."

"Where's my notebook?" said Farooqi, patting his many pockets. "I need a notebook. I want to journal this."

"There's a notebook over there," said Jake, trying to be helpful. "Under that half-empty bottle of soda."

"That's not a notebook. That's a coaster. Wait. I can use my phone. We can talk, and I'll record you."

Jake nodded. Recording was fine with him.

"Where's my phone?" said Farooqi. He stared at his guests.

Jake and Kojo glanced at each other.

"Are you asking us?" said Kojo.

"Of course I am!" said Farooqi. "Do you see anybody else in the room? Wait. Don't answer that. I sometimes see people who aren't really here. For instance, Albert Einstein and Marie Curie. They pop in sometimes. Tell me to keep on keepin' on."

"Cool," said Kojo. "I can dig it."

"Huh?" said Jake.

"That's from *Shaft*. He was big in the nineteen seventies, too."

"Okay," said Farooqi, nervously fidgeting his fingers in the air. "Never mind the notebook. Or the phone with the voice memo app. I don't need notes. Notes are overrated. Just tell me what happened after you ate my jelly beans. I'll remember. I'm good at remembering things."

"Yeah, like where he put his phone," Kojo muttered to Jake.

"Can I ask a question first?" said Jake.

"Yes, of course, young man," said Farooqi, stroking his chin thoughtfully, trying his best to look like a calm and wise scholar. "I'm sure you must have a lot of them."

"Are you a professor?"

Farooqi shook his head. "No. I'm a research assistant. Have been for nine years. This is my lab." He proudly gestured at everything in the cramped, cluttered room. "Nobody really bothers me. Ever. I think they forgot I'm down here. They still pay me, though. Not much. I eat a lot of ramen noodles. . . ."

"Um, sir?" said Kojo, pointing at the gurgling beaker of purple gunk. "Your purple goop is boiling over."

"I know that!" said Farooqi. "Now."

He twisted a green spigot on a gas tank.

"Forgot to turn off the Bunsen burner."

"A common piece of laboratory equipment that produces a single open flame," said Jake, "named after Robert Bunsen, who, in the eighteen fifties, with the help of the University of Heidelberg's chief mechanic, Peter Desaga, invented a prototype of a burner lamp designed to maximize temperature while minimizing luminosity."

Farooqi gawped at Jake. Tears welled up in his eyes.

"Oh my goodness. Zabardast! My jelly beans worked! I knew it. Isn't science amazing? Think of it! Oh, the wonder of what I have done!" He shook his fist at the ceiling, as if he were mad at somebody upstairs. "Ingestible Knowledge isn't just a theory, Dr. Blackbridge. Cognitive enhancement through the bloodstream is possible! This boy is proof! Living proof! I did it."

"But *how'd* you do it?" asked Kojo. " 'Cause I'm into science and—"

"What your friend here thought were jelly beans were actually sugar-coated nanoprogrammed capsules that can take your neural synapses back to what they were like when you were an infant learning everything at an astonishing rate, while simultaneously overloading those junctions with the chemical deposits associated with the learning of various subjects."

"Which jelly beans are good for basketball?" asked Kojo. "The green ones? The orange ones?"

"Basketball requires a complex combination of many diverse skills," said Farooqi. "I suspect that the rapid ingestion of a wide variety of Ingestible Knowledge pills—which, to tell you the truth, I was going to recommend that people take one at a time to master a specific subject—may have resulted in intelligence leaps and synaptic connections I never dreamed possible. The human brain is capable of so much. I just wanted to give it a gentle nudge!"

16

"**S**o what's the antidote?" asked Jake.

"Excuse me?" said Farooqi.

"The antidote. You know—the cure."

Now Farooqi looked confused. "You want a cure for the gift of superintelligence?"

"I don't know. Maybe. I'd like the option."

Kojo nodded. "He'd like the option."

"I see." Farooqi fidgeted with the sleeves of his lab coat. "Well, unfortunately, there isn't one."

"Excuse me?" said Jake and Kojo.

"They might wear off. You could lose your newfound intelligence. Eventually. Maybe all at once. Who knows? Not me. But I do know that there is no antidote. I wasn't sure what I was doing would work, so why on earth would I worry about inventing a way to reverse it if it did? I need your contact information."

"What for?" asked Jake.

"You're Subject One!"

"No, I'm not. I'm just Jake McQuade. I want to go back to being who I was."

"You mean the laziest dude in seventh grade?" said Kojo.

"I'm not lazy," said Jake defensively. "I prefer to think of myself as exertion-challenged." He turned to Farooqi. "Look, if you have the formulas for those jelly beans, you should be able to figure out some way to stop them from doing whatever they're doing inside my brain."

"Yeah. You'd think," said Farooqi. "Hey, I have an idea. Maybe *you* can design the antidote."

"What?"

"You're way smarter than me right now. I bet your IQ is off the charts. You want to take a test?"

"No. I want you to give me the formulas . . . or the formulae. Either is correct as the plural of *formula*."

"Oooh," said Kojo. "One of those jelly beans definitely had some grammar in it."

"I don't have the formulas or the formulae," said Farooqi.

"What?"

"I'm like the world's finest chefs. I improvise. A little bit of this. A dash of that. Oh, sure, like every good scientist, I eventually write my recipes down on three-by-five index cards and store them in a tin box, but I can't be constrained by rigid formulas or formulae. I'm an artist, not an automaton!" He took a moment to compose himself. "Of course, before I publish, I'll have to make certain I can replicate the results. Those are the rules of science. I didn't write them. I believe Sir Isaac Newton did. So, for now, let's not worry about an antidote. Let's think of all the incredible things we can do together. You're the smartest kid in the universe, Jake McQuade. Maybe you're the one who invents the warp drive engines for *Star Trek*. Or you could, you know, cure diseases. You could probably use your math skills to make a killing on Wall Street."

"I've got to go," said Jake.

"You'll allow me to follow you?" said Farooqi. "Take notes?"

"No!" said Jake. His head was spinning. "Not now. My mom has another banquet at the hotel tonight, and I have to fix dinner for my little sister because we are not going back to the Imperial Marquis to eat. That hotel has too many highly dangerous snack-food items lying around!"

17

Jake and Kojo retraced their bus routes back uptown.

Jake didn't help anyone with their homework. He didn't speak French, Swahili, or Mandarin to any tourists. He just pouted. And felt sorry for himself.

On the third bus, a man boarded with an open cardboard container of, judging by the aroma, Chinese food. Even though it was against all the posted rules and regulations, he started eating it. Fast.

And then the bus hit a bump.

The man started choking.

His face flushed red as both of his hands flew up to his neck. The open container tumbled out of his lap and hit the floor.

Jake saw it was chicken and cashews.

He sprang from his seat and raced to the gasping man, who couldn't talk but was making squeaky noises. Jake got behind the man, wrapped his arms around his belly, and gave five fist thrusts to the abdomen, pulling up as he yanked in to engage the diaphragmatic muscle.

Finally, a cashew popped out of the man's mouth. He started breathing again.

"Thank you," he said. "Good thing you know the Heimlich maneuver."

"Yeah," said Jake. "I guess so."

Jake went back to his seat.

Kojo was staring at him in astonished admiration.

"Dude, you're like Spider-Man."

"What?"

"For real. He got bit by a radioactive spider. You ate jelly beans. You both ended up with superpowers."

"But why me?"

"Because you ate the jelly beans! Fate put them there and you gobbled down your destiny."

"You think this is my destiny? To be super smart?"

Kojo shrugged. "I guess. Until the jelly beans wear off, anyway. But until they do, I think you need to use your Spidey powers to do whatever smart stuff needs doing."

Jake thought about what Kojo had just said.

And since he was suddenly super intelligent, he knew Kojo was right.

He'd been given a rare gift.

It was time to use it.

18

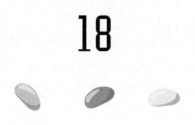

The next morning, on his way to school, Jake noticed a long line snaking out of the corner bodega, a small grocery and convenience store where people bought their coffee, bagels, and egg sandwiches.

Jake wanted to grab a doughnut, but he'd never seen a line so long.

"Is it the Mega Millions lotto?" Jake asked a woman at the end of the line. The bodega also sold lottery tickets.

"Nah," said the woman. "Their cash register is broken. They have to ring everybody up the old-fashioned way: figuring it out on paper."

"It's taking forever," groused a man, checking his watch.

"Excuse me," said Jake, making his way down the sidewalk.

"Hey, kid," someone shouted. "There's a line here. Where do you think you're going?"

"Inside to help," he replied. "Turns out, I'm pretty good at math."

Jake said a quick "Hi!" to Oliver, the store's cat, who was lying on his fuzzy blanket underneath the produce rack while scratching at his neck and jingling his collar.

Dominic, the guy who usually worked the register in the mornings, was pushing a pencil across the back of a brown paper bag. Jake went up on tiptoe so he could see Dominic's math scrawls.

"Okay, there's sales tax on the stuff that's not food. . . . Uh, eight times eight, carry the six . . ."

"The total is fifteen seventy-four," Jake told Dominic. "He has a twenty. You owe him four dollars and twenty-six cents."

Dominic gave Jake a quizzical look, then took the man's twenty and gave him the correct change.

Meanwhile, Jake scanned the next customer's items and did the math in his head, remembering to add sales tax to all non-food items.

"She's four thirty-two," Jake announced.

"I'd like a buttered roll," said the next person in line.

Surprise. It was Grace.

Jake smiled at her.

She gave him a puzzled look. "You work here?"

"Nah," said Jake. "Just trying to help out."

"So how much is a buttered roll and a juice?" Grace asked.

"Four twenty-five."

"And I want a pack of gum."

"Six thirty-three."

"No, make that a tin of mints."

"Seven eighteen."

"Forget the mints and the gum," said Grace. "Just the juice and buttered roll, but with extra butter."

"We're back to four twenty-five. They don't charge for extra butter."

"It's true," said Dominic. "We don't."

Grace paid, stepped aside, and waited for the lady behind the deli counter to slice, butter, and wrap her roll.

Jake went back to work as a human cash register. Grace sipped her juice, nibbled her roll, and, amazed, watched Jake blaze through a lightning round of addition, subtraction, multiplication, and division.

After two dozen more ring-ups, the morning rush was over. A repair person arrived to fix the store's cash register. Jake's job at the bodega was done.

"So tell me, Jake," said Dominic. "How'd you get so good at math?"

"Yeah," said Grace, finishing her buttered roll. "I was going to ask the same question."

Jake shrugged. "I dunno. Guess I've just been eating right."

Dominic and Grace both gave that answer a confused nod.

"Oh, and, Dom? You might want to take Oliver to the vet. Judging by the way he's scratching his neck and biting at his legs in a fast, frantic manner, I suspect he might need a flea bath."

Now Grace was squinting at Jake. "How'd you know *that*?"

"Easy. The cat was scratching his neck and biting his legs."

"Riiiight."

19

Grace and Jake walked to school together.

They didn't really talk. Grace said something like "Nice weather." Jake gave her the extended five-day forecast complete with information about the fluctuating barometric pressure. Grace didn't say anything after that.

Jake wondered if Haazim Farooqi might be able to create a jelly bean for talking to girls.

"See you later, Jake," said Grace when they hit the front doors. She was studying Jake's eyes. "There might be something we should talk about. We'll see."

"Um, okay."

Jake started sweating profusely and immediately knew why: when emotional stress causes a reaction from your sympathetic nervous system, it primarily affects the eccrine sweat glands on your face, your palms, and the soles of your feet, and in your armpits.

In other words, you get BO.

He wished he didn't know that, but he did.

Grace bopped up the hall to Mr. Lyons's homeroom. Jake tucked in his arms so no one could see his sweat balloons and went into Mr. Keeney's class.

As usual, the teacher was snoozing in his chair with his feet up on the desk. He was wearing a black T-shirt with bold white letters proclaiming 5 OUT OF 4 PEOPLE HAVE TROUBLE WITH MATH. Jake noticed a sci-fi paperback open in his lap. It rose up and down in time with his snores. There was also a *Star Wars* Yoda poster on the wall. Yoda was doing a math problem: SOLVE OR SOLVE NOT. THERE IS NO TRY IN MATH.

Jake wondered if the reason Mr. Keeney was so bored all the time was because no one ever asked him any interesting or challenging questions. Jake also wondered if boredom with everyday, humdrum things might be a curse that came with superintelligence. If so, he hoped the jelly beans wore off before it happened to him.

"Excuse me, Mr. Keeney," said Jake, gently waking him.

"What?" growled the groggy teacher.

"Is that book about aliens?"

"Yes. It's science fiction."

"Fascinating. What do you think would be humanity's reaction if we ever really discovered extraterrestrial life?"

Mr. Keeney sat up in his chair. He looked stunned. He shook his head, wiped some sleep out of his eyes, reached for his giant *Battlestar Galactica* travel mug, took a sip, and led his homeroom class in a fifteen-minute discussion on what he called the "philosophical ramifications of knowing that we're not alone in the universe."

Everyone agreed: it was the best homeroom period ever.

In social studies, in a unit on basic economics, Jake helped Mr. Lyons by describing the difference between satisfying wants and meeting needs to a group that just couldn't grasp the concept.

"A need is something a person has to have in order to thrive," he explained. "A want is a choice. For instance, we need to eat in order to live. So I need to eat breakfast every morning. But I might *want* to eat pizza for breakfast, even though I don't need to!"

After school, Jake and Kojo led the Riverview Pirates to their second basketball victory.

"Look at me, Jake," shouted Kojo right before he shot the buzzer beater to seal the game. "I'm putting up parabolas!"

Grace was in the bleachers, watching and cheering. She might've been taking notes, too.

That night, Jake cooked dinner for Emma because their mom had to work another banquet at the hotel. He whipped up a very colorful taco pizza based on a recipe he just seemed to know.

But later, when Emma asked him to help her with her Spanish homework, Jake drew a blank.

"Everybody says you're so smart at school all of a sudden," said his frustrated sister. "Why are you so dumb here at home?

Jake still no habla español.

If he wanted to help Emma, he would need another jelly bean.

20

On Saturday, Jake and Kojo rode the bus back to Warwick College.

"What's the use of being smart if I can't help Emma?" said Jake. "I need another jelly bean. For Spanish."

"To help Emma with her homework?" said Kojo, arching his eyebrows above the thick frames of his glasses. "Not so you can chat with Grace and drop some Spanish love bombs on her? Some more of that 'amo, amas, amat' action?"

"Grace and I are just friends, Kojo. And 'amo, amas, amat' is Latin, not Spanish, although Spanish is considered one of the romance languages."

"Uh-huh. That's what I'm talking about. *Romance*."

"We call Spanish a romance language, Kojo, because it, like Portuguese, French, Italian, and Romanian, originated from Latin, the language spoken in the western *Roman* Empire."

"Um-hmmm. Well, I call Spanish a romance language because that's what Grace speaks when she's making goo-goo eyes at you. Did you see her in the bleachers yesterday? She never used to come to our basketball games."

"Yes. That did strike me as a bit odd. I can't quite surmise why she was there."

"Dude?"

"Yes, Kojo?"

"You're starting to sound like a robot."

"Sorry. I just seem to precipitously have this capacious and voluminous vocabulary at my disposal."

"Doesn't mean you have to use it."

"Point taken."

"I figure Grace was at the game because she has a crush on you."

"A crush?"

"I've seen the way she's been looking at you ever since you jelly-beaned your way into superintelligence. She's super smart. Now you're even smarter than me. You two are a match made in nerd heaven."

When they reached Warwick College and, once again, made their way across campus to Haazim Farooqi's cluttered chemistry lab, Jake got right to the point.

"I need to speak Spanish, Mr. Farooqi. My little sister goes to a Spanish-immersion school. I want to be able to help her with her homework. I need a Spanish-language jelly bean."

"He also needs it to *communicate* with Grace Garcia," added Kojo, "if you know what I mean by *communicate*." Kojo gave the wild-looking scientist a wink and a nudge.

"It's not for Grace," said Jake.

"Is too."

"Is not."

"Too."

"Not."

Suddenly, the smartest kid in the universe and his superintelligent best friend sounded like kindergartners.

"Enough," said Farooqi, throwing up his arms in exasperation. "Fine. You want a Spanish-language jelly bean? I'll make you one. Because"—he put on a singsongy voice—"'that's what Jake wants.' Well, what about what I want?"

Farooqi whipped off his safety glasses, trying to look tough.

"Are you trying to look tough?" asked Kojo.

"Yes," Farooqi replied sheepishly.

"Not working, dude."

"I know. It never does. Anyway, what *I* want, Jake, is your full cooperation. We must become true partners in this enterprise so I can refine and replicate my formulas."

"Or formulae," said Jake.

"Right. Both are acceptable. You told me. This is one big step for you, Jake, but one giant leap for mankind."

"You're incorrectly paraphrasing Neil Armstrong," said Jake. "The first human to set foot on the moon."

"Indeed I am," said Farooqi. "But you only knew that's what I was doing because of my jelly beans!"

"Which one?" asked Kojo. "Because I wouldn't mind bumping up my trivia game . . ."

"We may never know which bean did what to your friend," Farooqi explained.

"I ate them all at once," added Jake. "It wasn't what is known as a controlled experiment. You see, Kojo, whenever possible, scientists like to test their hypotheses with a scientific test done under controlled conditions, meaning that just one or a few factors are changed at a time, while all others are kept constant."

"Which one gave him that last mouthful of gibberish?" asked Kojo. "Because I don't need that jelly bean. Probably the nasty-tasting licorice one . . ."

Farooqi didn't answer. He was too busy beaming at Jake. "Look what I hath wrought!"

Jake shook his head. "Now you're misquoting the Bible phrase that became the first Morse code message transmitted in the United States on May twenty-fourth, 1844!"

"Okay," said Kojo. "Now we're back to the trivia bean. That's the one I want. Was that the pink one? The red?"

"It doesn't matter which jelly bean did what," said

Farooqi. "I don't have any more prototypes left. Jake ate them all! Wiped out my entire supply. But I will attempt to craft more—including one that'll ensure your mastery of the Spanish language—if, Jake, you agree to let me study you. If you'll become Subject One in the scholarly paper I plan to start writing, as soon as I find my pen and a blank piece of paper."

Jake nodded and extended his hand.

He and Farooqi shook on it.

They had a deal.

"It might take me a little while to concoct this new chemical confection," said the scientist. "In the meantime, Jake, you should go to the library."

"Why? I already know everything I need to know."

"Except Spanish," said Kojo.

"Right. But Dr. Farooqi's going to make a pill for that."

"I'm not a doctor," said Haazim. "Not yet, anyway. But one day. Maybe. After I find that pen and write my paper. Plus there's no guarantee that my Spanish pill will perform as requested. However, Jake, if my theories are correct, your jelly bean–primed brain is ready to receive much more information—especially in the categories you've already begun to master. Even with the booster shot of my Ingestible Knowledge capsules, you haven't pushed your intelligence to the max, my young friend. To do that, you need to crack open a few books!"

21

Jake and Kojo went to the branch of the city's public library that Jake had never realized was less than a block away from his apartment building.

"When'd they put this here?" he remarked, admiring the three-story structure with gracefully arched windows and a strongly detailed roofline. (Apparently, architecture appreciation had been in one of the jelly beans he'd gobbled down, too.)

"Oh, not too long ago," said Kojo, pointing to the marble cornerstone. "I think it was back in *1912!*"

Jake and Kojo found a work desk up on the second floor.

"Here you go," said Kojo, setting down a stack of clothbound books. "Like Mr. Farooqi said, you should start with subjects you're already pretty good at. We'll wait for Spanish until after he finishes your new you-know-what. Okay—these are college math textbooks."

Jake opened the first book and, like a high-powered copy machine that drank way too much coffee, flipped through the pages in a flash.

"Done," he told Kojo. "Next book. Something meatier."

"What? You didn't read the whole book. . . ."

"Yes, I did."

"You were just skimming the pages. No way could you retain any knowledge."

"Oh, really? Well, if x is greater than or equal to zero, then x to the fourth power minus six times x squared plus nine equals the absolute value of x squared minus three."

Kojo nodded. Slowly. "Okay. If you say so."

"Bump me up to grad school–level stuff. Something Einstein would have trouble understanding."

For the next three hours, Kojo brought Jake books; Jake soaked them up into his jumbo-sized sponge of a brain.

A few library patrons started to watch. They were mesmerized by Jake McQuade, the human learning machine. Kojo wondered if he should charge admission. There had to be some way to cash in on Jake's newfound gift.

"We need to put you on *Jeopardy!*, baby!" Kojo blurted.

"Or," said a familiar voice, "you could just join me on the Quiz Bowl team."

It was Grace. She was carrying a leather-bound journal sealed inside a plastic zip-top bag.

"I'm in," said Kojo. "Sign me up."

"Hey, Grace," said Jake, feeling his sweat glands going into overdrive again. "Whatcha doin'?"

"Little research."

"'Bout what?"

Jake's massive vocabulary seemed to vanish whenever he talked to Grace.

"You ever heard of a pirate captain named Aliento de Perro?" Grace asked him.

Jake shook his head. Kojo, too.

"It's Spanish," explained Grace. "Means 'Dog Breath.' He was on a pirate ship that raided ports up and down the eastern seaboard back in the early seventeen hundreds. One of my mom's ancestors was on his crew. A guy named Eduardo Leones."

"Your ancestor worked for a guy named Dog Breath?" said Jake.

"Yep."

"I take it this particular pirate forgot to pack his mouthwash?" said Kojo.

"Actually," said Jake, "mouthwash wasn't invented until the late eighteen hundreds. . . ."

"How come you know that?" asked Grace.

Jake tapped one of the book heaps cluttering the work desk.

"Been studying."

"That's a math book," said Grace.

"We did a little dental hygiene history work, too," said Kojo.

"We did," said Jake. "For instance, did you know that the ancient Romans used bottles of urine as a refreshing oral rinse? They thought the ammonia in urine would disinfect mouths and whiten teeth."

Kojo scrunched up his face. "And I thought Listerine tasted bad. . . ."

Grace's deep brown eyes went wide. "You *have* to be on our team, Jake McQuade."

"Why?" wondered Kojo. "Will we get a lot of questions about gargling with pee?"

"No," said Grace. "But I've been watching you, Jake. You've changed. All of a sudden, you're . . . smart."

"Maybe," said Jake.

"You know all sorts of obscure facts."

"I guess. But it's not like I was born smart like you and Kojo."

"Excuse me?" chorused Grace and Kojo.

"You guys have been geniuses since kindergarten. You were born smart."

"Not me, baby," said Kojo.

"Me neither," said Grace. "We just work really, really hard. So do a lot of other kids at school. Something, it seems, you don't have to do."

"You're right," said Kojo, who sounded like he was about to reveal Jake's jelly bean secret to Grace. "That's because he—"

"Had a growth spurt," said Jake. "A brain growth spurt."

That made Grace laugh. "Seriously?"

"Yeah. Typically, leaps in mental development only happen to infants—when they're mastering major new cognitive and motor skills, like sitting or crawling. I think I had one of those. Just a little later than usual. I should probably see a doctor about it."

"Nah," said Grace. "You're twelve. Growth spurts happen."

"Yeah."

"So, Jake, will you *please* join Kojo and me on the Quiz Bowl team? ¿Por favor?"

"I don't know. . . ."

"The school needs you! *I* need you."

When Grace said that, Kojo wiggle-waggled his eyebrows knowingly at Jake.

And Jake's face turned pink.

22

Patricia Malvolio was helping her uncle, Heath Huxley, set up a presentation in the boardroom of his midtown office building.

She propped the foam-board-mounted artist's rendering of his next towering condominium project on an easel.

"It's amazing, Uncle Heath!" she gushed. "Absolutely amazing."

"I know. It's huge!"

Mrs. Malvolio's eyes watered. She wished her uncle wouldn't use words with *H* in them. They sent out a lot of air. Foul air.

"Don't you just love the name I came up with? River-view Tower. Because it's a tower. With a river view."

"It's brilliant, Uncle Heath. I mean, who wouldn't want to live in a river-view tower? I know I'm looking forward to my free penthouse apartment. Care for a mint?"

"No thank you." He rubbed his hands together. "Some big spenders with deep pockets are dropping by this afternoon to take a peek. We're also opening up a showroom on East Eighty-Eighth Street with a model unit. I predict we'll presell ninety percent of the condos before we even break ground."

"Speaking of ground," said Mrs. Malvolio, "you should have it soon enough. We're still on track to be declared the district's worst middle school building. There're a few new leaks in the ceiling, and the health inspector finally wrote us up for those faulty refrigerators in the cafeteria. They're going to tear us down for sure!"

"When will the wrecking ball show up?"

"Hopefully this summer." She paused. A pained look crossed her face and crinkled her makeup.

"What's wrong?" asked Mr. Huxley, seeing her frown. "Your lipstick is cracking."

"Well, Uncle Heath, there's this one girl, Grace Garcia. . . ."

"What's the problem?"

"She's too smart. I tried to transfer her to Sunny Brook, but she refused. She could ruin all our plans. If that kind of brilliance can shine inside our shabby building, the city may refuse to tear the place down."

"Get rid of her, Patricia!"

"I'm working on it! But the girl is stubborn. Just like her uncle, my so-called vice principal, Charley Lyons. I've tried to encourage him to leave Riverview, too. Even made a few calls to set him up with a higher-paying job at Chumley Prep. He said, 'No thanks. Someone from my family has always worked at this school because we honor and cherish its history.' Blah, blah, blah."

Panic swirled in Mr. Huxley's eyes. "Do you think this Charley Lyons knows what we know?"

"I doubt it."

"He'd better not," said Mr. Huxley. "I paid good money for that information."

"It was a wise investment, Uncle Heath."

"Indeed it was, Patricia. Because I'm going to completely finance this tower with what we find in the caves underneath your ramshackle old school!"

Then he and Mrs. Malvolio laughed their sinister family laugh.

23

"Okay, Jake," said Kojo. "Here's your schedule for today."

"My schedule?"

"Yeah. I organized it on a spreadsheet so, you know, it would look all official and you wouldn't get confused like you did yesterday."

"I wasn't confused, Kojo. I was mad at you."

"Which was a remarkably dumb emotion for someone as smart as you and your jelly bean brain."

"I don't want to do other people's homework."

"Of course you don't. Not for free. That's why I've set up a fee structure."

"Fee structure?"

"Exactly. Let me run it down for you."

It was early in the morning. Before homeroom. Kojo and Jake were in the cafeteria with the last two chocolate milks they could find in the cooler.

"Now," said Kojo, "if some kid wants you to solve a math problem, that's five bucks. Or something really good from their lunch. You know—Ho Hos, Ding Dongs, Twinkies, something like that. If they need you to write, say, a whole essay for them, well, now we're talking ten, twenty dollars. I, of course, take my fifteen percent commission off the top. . . ."

"Fifteen percent?"

"I'm your agent. It's what we get." Kojo swiped his finger across his smartphone. "As you'll see, I've put together a pretty tight schedule for today. You have appointments at every class break."

"Hey, guys!" Grace breezed into the cafeteria. Her smile was bright. So were her eyes. "I thought we should have our first team meeting today. Now, I know you guys usually have basketball practice after school, so I'm thinking we can practice during lunch."

"Um, sorry," said Kojo, scrolling down his phone's screen. "Jake already has a lunch."

"Oh," said Grace. "Okay. How about fifth period? We all have specials. We could meet in the library."

"Nope," said Kojo. "No can do." He turned to Jake. "You have a deep-dive social studies paper that's due first thing tomorrow."

"You do?" said Grace. "We're in the same social studies class. I don't remember Uncle Charley saying anything about a paper being due tomorrow."

"Oh, it's not Jake's paper," said Kojo. "It's for Chase

Farnsworth. He's paying top dollar. Thirty bucks, on account of the fast turnaround."

"You're doing other kids' homework?" said Grace, looking seriously disappointed. "And getting paid for it?"

"Hey," said Kojo, "don't get all jealous. Just because we thought of doing it before you did . . ."

"I would never charge someone who needed help," said Grace defensively.

"Yeah," said Kojo. "We need to talk about that. You keep taking on charity cases, you're gonna drive down the fair market value of my man's brain."

Grace looked at Jake like she didn't know who he was.

"Are you really going to do this? Charge people to help them study? ¡No puedo creerlo!"

"I'm sorry," said Jake. "I don't know what you just said."

"Too bad. For a smart guy, you sure have a lot to learn."

Jake stood up. "I'm not going to charge people or do their homework for them. This side hustle was Kojo's idea."

"You mean this genius move was my idea," said Kojo. "And it's not a side hustle. It's our college tuition fund."

Jake ignored him. "I just came in here for a cold chocolate milk, which, by the way, I suspect was stored at a temperature well above the safety limit of forty degrees Fahrenheit. That's why it's so thick and chunky, Kojo."

"Huh," said Kojo. "So it's *not* a chocolate milkshake in a convenient cardboard carton?"

"No."

"Good thing we didn't drink any."

Jake shook his head and walked away.

"Where are you going?" Kojo hollered.

"I don't know," said Jake. "I need to clear my brain! Get out of my head. Do something physical. Maybe I'll go shoot some hoops or see if the janitor needs help sweeping the hallways."

"Mr. Schroeder isn't sweeping anything today," Grace shouted after Jake. "Mrs. Malvolio just fired him."

24

Jake slowly turned around.

"She fired Mr. Schroeder?" he said, sounding stunned, like his whole world was putrefying faster than the curdled chocolate milk he'd almost just drunk. "Why?"

"Our principal thinks we don't need a janitor," said Grace. "She told Uncle Charley that having Mr. Schroeder clean up after students is sending the wrong signal. She thinks we need to learn to clean up after ourselves."

"I guess she has a point," muttered Kojo.

"Uncle Charley is hasta el último pelo with Mrs. Malvolio."

"Huh?" said Jake.

"He's totally fed up with her. His father and grandfather were both custodians here. Someone from the

Lyons family has always worked on this plot of land, ever since the seventeen hundreds."

"This school's that old?" said Kojo.

"There wasn't always a school on this property," said Jake. "First it was a farm. And then a warehouse for goods being shipped down the river. A school wasn't built until the early nineteen hundreds."

"That's right," said Grace.

"But the school's had a custodian since day one. Am I right?" said Kojo.

"It's traditional," said Jake.

"And sanitary," added Grace.

Jake smiled. He liked when Grace finished his thoughts for him.

"But now," said Kojo, "they just up and fire the janitor because they want us to pick up our own trash?"

"That's not the real reason," said Grace. "It's just another part of Mrs. Malvolio's scheme. If the school looks disgusting, if the place is a mess, if garbage is piled up in the halls and the toilets are all clogged, the school board will shut Riverview down."

Kojo nodded. "I read somewhere that they need to close one middle school this year. Tear down the building . . ."

"Well," said Grace, "according to Uncle Charley, Mrs. Malvolio wants them to sell *this* property. To her uncle, who just happens to be Heath Huxley."

"Oooh," said Kojo. "That dapper and dashing dude is a real estate tycoon! I've seen his commercials on TV."

"He's also in Mrs. Malvolio's office right now."

"Then let's roll," said Kojo, sticking a Tootsie Pop in his mouth. "We need to do a little detective work."

25

"I've got it!" said Mrs. Malvolio, springing up out of her rolling chair.

Its wheels wobbled. Like everything else at Riverview Middle, the chair probably should've been replaced decades ago.

Her uncle remained seated in the office's sagging visitor's chair. It was hard to stand once you'd sunk into its squishy foam rubber cushions.

The two of them had been brainstorming ways to speed up the demolition of Riverview Middle School.

"What's the big idea?" asked Heath Huxley.

"We host the District Middle School Quiz Bowl!"

"And how does that help our humble cause?"

Mrs. Malvolio nonchalantly fanned the air. Her uncle's last sentence had three stinky *H*s in it.

"It's a great opportunity to showcase this building's

horrible condition. Especially now that I've fired the janitor. Representatives from all the other schools in the district would be here. So would most of the school board members. Garbage will be piled up in the hallways and the cafeteria. The toilets will be clogged with paper towels and worse. If we host the Quiz Bowl, the superintendent might close us down and bring in the wrecking ball before the school year is even over."

Mr. Huxley worked his way out of the lumpy chair.

"I like where you're going with this, Patricia," he said.

"Thank you." She touched her hand to her heart. "I was hoping you might."

"Oh, it's a terrific plan. It could really ramp up our timetable. Get us to our financing source sooner. I just have one concern. One qualm."

"Go on."

"This girl you told me about. The smart one."

"Grace Garcia? Not a problem."

"But if, by hosting this Quiz Bowl, you show the soft-headed world that Riverview Middle isn't a completely hopeless case, that children, like this Grace Garcia, can learn and thrive here, despite the wretched state of the building, they may not let us tear it down."

"Don't worry. I'll find a way to limit Grace's involvement on the big night."

"And how do you plan to do that?"

"I'm not sure. I have a sneaking suspicion that she might not be feeling very well when it's Riverview's turn to play."

26

Jake, Kojo, and Grace hurried up the halls, hoping to gather some intelligence about their foes: Mrs. Malvolio and her uncle, Heath Huxley.

Backpacks were piled on the floor because most of the lockers were busted. *They might stay glued there,* Jake thought. Without a janitor swishing a mop and swabbing the decks, the floor felt extremely gummy. Jake's rubber-soled shoes were making sticky *thwick* sounds with every step.

He shook his head when he passed a poster taped to a wall:

THIS IS NOW A JANITOR-FREE SCHOOL!
KINDLY CLEAN UP YOUR OWN MESSES
AND TAKE ALL TRASH, GARBAGE,
AND RECYCLABLES HOME WITH YOU.

A smiling Heath Huxley, his perfectly proportioned teeth shining like a white picket fence, stepped out of the principal's office and stroked his sleek black mane.

"That's him," whispered Kojo. "Heath Huxley. Real estate tycoon."

"Let's go say hello," Grace whispered back.

The trio hurried up the corridor.

"Hello, Miss Garcia," said Mrs. Malvolio.

"Hello, Mrs. Malvolio."

"We were just talking about you."

"Ah," said Mr. Huxley, stroking his chin and studying Grace as if she were a bug on the wall that he didn't quite know how to squish. "You're the brainy one. Patricia told me all about you. Congratulations."

Mrs. Malvolio fiddled with her chunky necklace. "So, Grace, have you put together your Quiz Bowl team?"

"Almost."

"I'm on board," said Kojo.

"Excellent," the principal said with a sly smile and a flickering series of eyelash flutters. "Perhaps Mr. McQuade here could be your third teammate."

Jake was about to say he might do it if Mrs. Malvolio rehired the janitor. But with a quick look, Grace told him not to.

"I'm, you know, thinking about it" was all Jake said.

"Wonderful," said Mrs. Malvolio, stifling a giggle. "Have a good day, children. And if you're late to class, don't worry about it. Take time to smell the roses . . . and whatever else might be rotting in the hallways."

Then Mrs. Malvolio and Mr. Huxley turned to walk away.

"That boy is a lazy fool," Jake heard Mrs. Malvolio whisper to her uncle. "This is so perfect. . . ."

Jake was about to protest when Grace put her hand on his arm.

It felt nice.

"Don't worry about what she says. We don't want Mrs. Malvolio to know how smart you've become. Not yet. If she does, she might try to sabotage all of us."

"What would be her reasoning?" asked Jake.

"When we win the Quiz Bowl, we'll also be showing the world that Riverview Middle School has a resident genius. . . ."

"You?"

"No, Jake—*you*. If the people in charge see that a student like you can come out of a place like this, maybe they won't let those two creeps tear us down."

"What about me?" said Kojo. "You think Mrs. Malvolio's afraid of me, too?"

"She should be," said Jake. "Because you're not only smart, you're the detective who is going to learn the truth about what those two are plotting."

Kojo grinned at his friend. "Who loves ya, baby?"

"You?"

"That's right, Jake. The three of us? We're like the Avengers or something. We're gonna save this school!"

"So, Jake, will you be on our team?" said Grace.

Jake's cell phone thrummed. He checked the screen. Haazim Farooqi had just hit him up with a text:

> Operation FRIJOL DE JALEA is complete.
> See you after school.

Jake figured *frijol de jalea* was Spanish for "jelly bean." (He still couldn't read or speak Spanish. He just recognized the word *frijol* from the refried beans on the menu at his mom's favorite Mexican restaurant.)

"Maybe," said Jake. "Probably. We'll see. I need to do some stuff at home this weekend. If that works out, then yeah. You know, maybe."

Grace rolled her eyes and walked away, muttering something under her breath in Spanish.

Jake had no idea what she was saying.

But he sure wished he did.

He really, really, really needed Farooqi's frijol de jalea.

27

When the final bell rang, Jake and Kojo bolted for the exit.

On the bus ride downtown to Warwick College, they both fired off quick texts to their moms explaining where they were (emergency basketball practice).

"Here it is!" said Farooqi. He was in his subbasement lab holding up a small plastic bag with one speckled purple jelly bean sealed inside. "As requested, this'll help you understand and speak Spanish. I think."

"You *think*?" said Jake.

"There are no guarantees when you're pushing the outer limits of science as I'm attempting to do. I'm conjuring up magic here, fellas. Put on your patience pants. It took me all week to cook up this one jelly bean. I had to tweak the growth factors."

"The what?" said Kojo.

Jake turned to his friend. "Learning happens when

brain cells make new connections. The strength of these connections is enhanced by a group of proteins in the brain called growth factors."

"He's absolutely right," said Farooqi.

"Of course he is," muttered Kojo. "He ate all the jelly beans. Didn't save any for me . . ."

Jake shrugged. "I didn't know they were smart pills when I ate them."

"Specific growth factors," said Farooqi, cutting off Kojo and Jake, "such as BDNF, a member of the neurotrophin family, encourage the growth of new neurons and synapses."

Now even Jake was staring at Farooqi.

"So that's your secret sauce?" said Kojo. "BDNF? What's it stand for? Brain diesel fuel?"

"You forgot the 'N,'" said Jake.

"Yeah. I couldn't come up with anything good for it. . . . Thought 'nuclear' would be too much . . ."

"'BDNF' stands for 'brain-derived neurotrophic factor,'" explained Farooqi. "And, yes, manipulating those proteins is the key to my research."

"Works for me," said Kojo. "Go for it, baby."

Jake nodded. Farooqi carefully peeled open the plastic bag's tiny zip top. He extracted the speckled purple jelly bean with a pair of stainless-steel tweezers. He glanced at the dive watch on the wrist of his free hand.

"Subject One is ingesting Spanish booster at four-oh-two p.m.," he said out loud. "I guess I should've turned on my recorder before I said that."

"I'll write it down for you," said Kojo.

"Thank you. Jake?"

Jake held out his hand. Farooqi dropped the jelly bean into his palm. Jake closed his eyes and popped the pellet into his mouth.

"Mmmmm. Tastes like Dr Pepper."

"I borrowed the idea from Jelly Bellys," Farooqi admitted.

"How long till Jake starts speaking Spanish?" asked Kojo.

"How long did it take after your first dose to feel the effects?" asked Farooqi.

"I don't know. Ten minutes? I was riding home on the bus. . . ."

"Then go!" said Farooqi. "Quick. Do it again. There might've been something about the stomach agitation generated by the bus ride that stimulated the chemical's rapid entry into your bloodstream and your remarkable results. Anything is possible when pursuing the impossible!"

Kojo and Jake grabbed their backpacks and headed for the door.

Farooqi dug an index card out of his lab coat.

"Llámame," he read off the card, "cuando empieces a hablar español."

"Huh?" said Jake.

"My friend Polo taught me how to say that," Farooqi explained. "It means, 'Call me when you start speaking Spanish'!"

28

"I need to hop off," said Jake when the bus was two stops away from his apartment building. "I want to procure some provisions."

"Huh?"

"Foodstuffs."

"Oh. You mean you're going grocery shopping?"

"Yeah. Sorry about my word choice. But I suddenly have an urge to whip up a feast of hot and cold appetizers for Mom and Emma."

"Before you do," said Kojo, "can you read that poster?" He gestured toward a print ad for Roach Motel written in Spanish above the rear exit door.

"Sure," said Jake. " 'Las cucarachas entran, pero no pueden salir.' "

"What's it mean?"

"Basically, it means, 'Roaches check in, but they don't check out.'"

Kojo's eyes lit up. "You can speak Spanish! The purple jelly bean worked."

"Not yet," said Jake. "I just remember the classic Roach Motel slogan that, apparently, the poster is attempting to repurpose for a Latinx audience. Catch you later, Kojo!"

Jake bounded off the bus.

Since he had the credit card his mother gave him "for groceries only," he zipped through the aisles of the cramped market and grabbed everything he knew he needed to create Spanish tapas!

Once home, he flew into a frenzy of slicing, dicing, and broiling.

"What are you doing?" asked Emma.

"Making dinner for us."

"Tapas?"

"Yeah. Pan tumaca con jamón, or tomatoes and ham on toasted bread, a Spanish omelet, plus some prawns with chorizo for me and Mom; olives, cheeses, vegan meatballs, and patatas bravas covered with a spicy sauce for vegetarian you."

"'Patatas bravas' means 'spicy or fierce potatoes,'" said Emma, dipping her finger in the sauce to give it the quick-lick taste test.

"Really?" said Jake, realizing he still didn't understand

Spanish, even if he did now know how to cook Spanish food better than the kids on *MasterChef Junior.*

When Jake's mother got home from work, she was so impressed by the gourmet meal that greeted her, she didn't ask anything about how much it cost.

"Who are you?" she asked. "And what have you done with my son?"

Jake grinned.

"I'm glad you're enjoying dinner."

"So where'd you learn to cook like this?" his mom asked when she finally pushed back from the table. Her plates held nothing but a few crispy crumbs.

"I'm not really sure."

"Probably TV," said Emma. "There are a lot of cooking shows on TV, and Jake watches a lot of TV."

"Yeah," said Jake. "I used to."

"Well, hon, I like this new you. You even made your bed this morning."

"I guess it's like Admiral William McRaven, the former head of the US Special Operations Command, said in a 2014 commencement speech, 'If you make your bed every morning, you will have accomplished the first task of the day. It will give you a small sense of pride, and it will encourage you to do another task and another and another.'"

Jake's mom smiled and stared at him.

"I ask again: Who are you?"

Jake laughed. "I'm still me, Mom," he told her (silently adding *sort of* in his head).

But it felt good.

Having his mom beaming at him with pride.

"Well, this was such a treat," said Mom. "This food was better than anything you could possibly find at the top tapas restaurants in Barcelona."

"You mean 'Barthelona,'" said Jake. "In the variety of Spanish spoken in Catalonia, where, of course, Barthelona is located, it is pronounced 'Barthelona.'"

"Thank you, Jake. I did not know that. I also did not know that, since you're such an expert on Spanish, you can now help Emma with her homework—instead of me." And then she speared a bite of patatas bravas from Emma's plate and popped it into her mouth. "Delicious, hon. Thanks again."

"Sí," said Emma. "Muy delicioso y considerado de tu parte, Jake."

And Jake still had no idea what she was saying.

29

After dinner, Jake went to his room and called Farooqi.

"This is Subject One," he said.

"Greetings, Subject One!" said Farooqi. "What's the report?"

"Failure to launch."

"The purple jelly bean didn't work?"

"Not the way we wanted it to. But my mom sure enjoyed my newfound mastery of Spanish cuisine. I also know some obscure historical trivia about Spain, the Spanish Armada, and, for some reason, Spaniels."

"Remarkable," said Farooqi. "But still no language skills?"

"Nada."

"That's Spanish! You just spoke Spanish."

"Everybody knows 'nada' means 'nothing.' It's been in movies."

"Okay, okay. I need to tweak the formula. Maybe lose the Dr Pepper flavoring. That might've thrown things off. Or not. It's a possibility. Sort of. I should've written the formula down somewhere. . . ."

"You don't know what you gave me?"

"I did. But then, when everything was bubbling in the test tube, I had a brainstorm. I added a secret ingredient."

"What was it?"

"I can't tell you, Jake. It's a secret."

"But you added it to the formula, right? You wrote it down?"

"No, Jake. I was having a brainstorm. You don't waste time writing things down when there's a storm raging in your brain!"

"Are all scientists as absentminded as you, Mr. Farooqi?"

"No. Only the good ones. Sir Isaac Newton. Nikola Tesla. Albert Einstein. Haazim Farooqi."

"That's you."

"I know. I'll be in touch."

Jake hung up. There was a knock on his door.

It was Emma.

"Can you help me? I'm having trouble with my verbs."

"Ah, yes. Verbs. A word used to describe an action, state, or occurrence that forms the main part of the predicate in a sentence. To run. To sprint. To dart. To dash. To scuttle . . ."

"These are Spanish verbs."

"Okay. Hopefully they still describe an action, et cetera."

"I don't know when to use 'ser' and when to use 'estar.' "

And neither did Jake.

"Hold that thought, Emma," he told his little sister. "Help is on the way."

And then he made another phone call. To Grace.

Grace, who had already finished her homework, came over right away. Jake's mother offered her dessert.

"Would you like one of the torrejas Jake made for dinner? They're very cinnamony. Like Spanish French toast!"

"No thank you, Ms. McQuade."

"Call me Michelle. You kids have fun. I need another torreja. . . ."

Mom went back to the kitchen. Grace and Jake went to Emma's room, where Emma was frowning at a Spanish-language worksheet. Jake watched in amazement as Grace clearly explained the difference between the two verbs.

"They both mean 'is.' But use 'ser' for something that's permanent—like your black hair. Use 'estar' for something that can change—like your confusion about these two verbs. For instance, if you want to say 'I'm in love with you,' you'd use the first-person singular form of 'estar'—'estoy'—because that's something that can change. Over time. The more you get to know someone . . ."

Jake started tugging at his shirt collar. Emma's bedroom was amazingly toasty all of a sudden. Like the radiator was overheating.

Grace drilled Emma on a series of sample sentences. Emma caught on quickly. Thirty minutes later, she hugged Grace and then she hugged Jake.

"Thanks for having such smart friends," she said. "Thanks, Grace!"

"De nada, Emma," said Grace.

And Jake actually understood what she meant.

30

"Thanks for coming over," Jake told Grace.

"My pleasure. It's really hard to learn on your own. We all need help."

True, thought Jake. *And some of us also need jelly beans.*

"I'd better head home," Grace announced. "I took the bus."

"Let me walk you to the stop."

Jake and Grace rode the elevator down to the lobby. That made Jake all kinds of nervous. He tried to will the sweat glands in his armpits to take a break.

They didn't listen.

His brain wasn't *that* good.

"You really speak Spanish beautifully," he told Grace, his voice cracking slightly.

"Thanks. My mom and dad came to America from

Cuba. We still speak Spanish in my house . . . and English, of course."

"I'm better with English."

They exited the building and headed up the block.

"You know, Jake," said Grace, "if you really want to understand and speak Spanish, you could just *study* Spanish."

"Yeah. I've heard that works. For some people."

"So how'd you get so smart so fast if you didn't study?"

"Um . . ."

For some reason—maybe embarrassment, maybe because he was afraid she wouldn't believe him—Jake wasn't ready to tell Grace the truth. About Haazim Farooqi. About the jelly beans. About any of it.

"I don't know," he told her. "It just sort of happened. . . . Hey, do you know why we're called the Riverview Pirates? Because—BOOM!—I just figured it out."

"Oh, you did, did you?"

"Either that or a synapse in my brain just got a fresh shot of BDNF."

"Huh?"

"Nothing. But that pirate you told us about, Captain Dog Breath, he was chased upriver by the British, the same guys who defeated the Spanish Armada in 1588. Legend has it Dog Breath docked his ship very close to where our school now stands."

Grace stared into Jake's eyes. Like she was sizing him up. Seeing if she could trust him with what she said next.

113

"The boat that docked near where the school stands today wasn't Dog Breath's *El Perro Apestoso*."

"What's that mean?"

" 'The *Stinky Dog*.' "

"Cool."

"It was a rowboat piloted by the ship's Cubano cabin boy, Eduardo Leones. He found a cave. A place to hide the ship's treasure so the British couldn't seize it. He also didn't want Dog Breath to find it, because the evil captain had made Eduardo's father, Angel Vengador Leones, the *real* captain of the pirate ship, walk the plank after an ugly mutiny."

"How do you know all this? Because I don't have any of it." Jake tapped the sides of his head the way some people do when the TV is getting bad reception.

"Not many people know about the cabin boy. Or his father. Or the treasure. Just everybody in my family. Including Uncle Charley. He and my mom are both direct descendants of Angel and Eduardo Leones. 'Leones' means 'lions' in Spanish."

"It does? I mean, when you say it like that, 'Leones' kind of sounds like 'lions.' "

"Uncle Charley's great-great-grandparents just changed the spelling a little, to L-y-o-n-s. Jake, there's a reason why a member of our family has worked on that plot of land for over three centuries. They've been there to guard the cabin boy's buried treasure!"

"So there's really treasure? Underneath the school? Pirate treasure?!"

Jake was so excited, it made Grace laugh.

"Sí."

"Of course!" said Jake. "Your uncle Charley's father and grandfather were *custodians* at Riverview. 'Someone employed to clean and maintain a building' is only the *second* definition of that word. The first is 'a person who has responsibility for or looks after something.' Custodians are protectors."

Grace nodded. "For centuries, members of my family have served as noble knights, guarding the treasure our ancestors bequeathed to us."

"But wait a second—why didn't your uncle or one of those other ancestors dig up the treasure if they all knew where it was hidden?"

"Oh, they've tried. Many times. Uncle Charley went on a few expeditions with his father, who'd gone treasure hunting with his father. But the cabin boy was very, very clever. He hid the treasure where no one could find it, not even his family, unless they could decipher his complicated and confusing clue."

"So the treasure is still there?" said Jake. "Underneath the school?"

"Yep," said Grace. "And if Mrs. Malvolio and Mr. Huxley bulldoze the building, if they reduce it to rubble and crush the cave entrance, we may never be able to find it."

"Then we need to stop them. You're right, Grace. We need to put on a good show at the Quiz Bowl. Impress people with the education ordinary kids like you and me are receiving at Riverview Middle. That might stop the wrecking ball. . . ."

"So you'll join my team?"

"Sí," said Jake. "That's Spanish. For 'yes'!"

Grace grinned. "Is that so? Well, you learn something new every day."

"Hey, I know I do. Usually several things. All at once . . ."

"But, Jake?"

"Yeah?"

"Remember: We can't let Mrs. Malvolio know how brilliant you've become. She can't know you're our secret weapon. I need you to act dumb at school."

"No problem. I've had a lot of practice doing that."

31

When Jake and Grace arrived at school the next morning, Kojo was waiting for them.

"In here. I picked up some hot intel."

He motioned for Grace and Jake to follow him into an empty classroom.

Grace closed the door.

"What'd you find out?" she asked.

"That you are absolutely, one hundred percent correct, Grace. Mr. Huxley plans on tearing down our school and building a high-rise condominium. He calls it Riverview Tower. Because it's a tower. With a river view. They've set up a showroom over on East Eighty-Eighth Street. You can walk around in a model apartment. There's an artist's rendering of what the building will look like, and it looks like it's standing right on top of where our school's supposed to be."

Jake sank down on a stool. "Then it's hopeless. If they're that far along."

"Nothing's hopeless until you give up hope," said Grace.

"You really think that we can stop them?"

"Of course we can. If we use our brains, anything's possible!"

"But," said Jake, "Huxley has money and power. He has Mrs. Malvolio."

"And we have you, Jake," said Grace. "For some reason, through whatever kind of miracle, you've been given a gift."

"I didn't ask for it."

"Sometimes the best gifts are the ones you weren't expecting."

"That's true," said Kojo. "My last birthday? My mom gave me a kitten from the animal shelter. I didn't ask for a kitten. Now? I love Squeaky. That's her name."

"Awww," said Grace. "Cute."

"Yeah. She squeaks when she meows."

Grace looked Jake straight in the eye. Her eyes were deep and soulful. His armpits were damp and moist.

"Jake," she said, "we need to save the school and whatever my ancestor buried underneath it."

"Whoa," said Kojo. "There's something buried underneath the school?"

"Allegedly," said Jake.

"Pirate booty," said Grace.

"You mean gold doubloons or those cheesy corn puffs?"

"Gold doubloons, jewels, silver," said Grace. "A whole treasure chest filled with plunder."

"Dude?" Kojo said to Jake. "We gotta do this thing. Sure, we're the underdogs. The small fries in the McDonald's of life. But if we dig up that treasure chest, we'll have some serious coinage."

"Actually, it kind of belongs to my family," said Grace. "Legend has it that the pirate Dog Breath stole it all from our noble ancestor Angel Vengador Leones, who was a brave buccaneer."

"Okay, how about a fifteen percent commission for me and Jake?" said Kojo. "I want somebody to give me fifteen percent of something."

"Five," said Grace.

"Twelve," countered Kojo.

"Seven."

"Ten!"

Grace nodded. "That would work."

"You guys?" said Jake. "Don't focus on the treasure. Not yet. First we have to stop Heath Huxley from tearing down our school."

"Right," said Grace.

"For now," added Kojo. "But then we're moving into that ten percent territory. . . ."

A speaker tucked into a corner of the ceiling started to cackle and hum.

"Is this thing on?" said Mrs. Malvolio's voice. "It is?"

There was a series of thuds as the principal tapped the microphone.

"Been so long since we used this darn thing," she mumbled.

Grace, Kojo, and Jake glanced at each other.

"Something's up," said Kojo.

"Attention, students. This is Mrs. Malvolio. May I have your attention? I have a very important announcement. I am pleased to report that, for the first time ever, our school will be hosting the district-wide Quiz Bowl competition. It will take place next Thursday night in our gymnasium. If you are interested in participating, contact Grace Garcia, who has volunteered to be the captain of our three-person squad. That is all. Have a nice day."

"We're hosting?" said Grace. "We've never hosted. Something's up." She turned to Jake. "You're definitely in?"

He nodded. "Yeah. Definitely."

"Then I'd better go tell Mrs. Malvolio I already have my teammates!"

32

For the next few days, Jake focused on not revealing his newfound brainpower.

He pretended that he didn't know that the square root of four was two.

"How can a number have roots?" he told Mr. Keeney, the homeroom teacher who was also his math instructor. "It's not a tree."

Mr. Keeney closed his eyes and pinched the top of his nose. "You were so smart," he muttered. "Yesterday."

Jake even went back to playing basketball the way he used to. Badly. With lots of two-handed, underarm tosses. Except at the foul line, because jelly bean–brain Jake knew that a scientific analysis had concluded that using a "granny-style" technique was the optimal method for making a free throw, and, until after the Quiz Bowl, he had to miss those shots, too.

His mom was proud to hear that Jake had joined the Quiz Bowl team. His sister was worried.

"Everybody at the bus stop says you're dumb again," she told him.

Finally, on Thursday night, Jake, Kojo, and Grace put on matching black polo shirts and Pittsburgh Pirates baseball caps. They marched into the gymnasium to meet their competition—Quiz Bowl teams from the five other middle schools in the district.

Jake, of course, was nervous. His stomach, queasy. What if this turned out to be the exact moment the jelly beans wore off?

The bleachers were packed. Jake's mom and Emma were there. Emma was nervously fidgeting with her hair and chewing the tips. His mom was beaming again. In fact, Jake's mom had been smiling and tearing up ever since he told her he was on the school's Quiz Bowl team.

"I'm so, so proud of you," she'd gushed.

Haazim Farooqi was in the audience, too. He couldn't wait to see Subject One performing under pressure.

And the pressure was enormous.

"That's the district superintendent of schools," Grace whispered as they crossed the gym's hardwood floor.

"Where?" asked Jake.

"The lady with the glasses sitting next to my dad."

"Your dad's the guy with the goatee in the turtleneck and sport coat?"

"Yeah. He's a college professor. He has to look like that. It's a rule."

"TV's here, too," said Kojo excitedly, nodding toward a couple of camera crews from local stations that had set up their tripods and equipment on the gym floor. "I love watching TV. Now I'm gonna be *on* TV!"

Great, thought Jake. *Now everyone can watch me mess up. And if they have a DVR, they can rewind and watch me do it again!*

A podium stood in the center circle of the basketball court. It was flanked by two cloth-covered tables with three chairs and one microphone each. Max Myer, the meteorologist at one of the local TV stations, was checking himself in a hand mirror, prepping and primping to be the celebrity quizmaster.

"You kids ready to do us proud?" asked Mrs. Malvolio when she came over to greet the three Riverview Pirates. She was carrying a plate of brownies loosely covered with plastic wrap. "Here. The PTO baked these for you."

"Thanks," said Grace, grabbing two. Then a third. "Do we have a PTO?"

"Not really," said Mrs. Malvolio. "I shut it down. But if we *did* have a PTO, I'm sure they'd want to thank you for what you kids are doing. Take the whole plate. They're yours. You'd better find your seats. We're about to start. Eat more brownies, kids. You're not on until the third round."

She smiled at Jake. "Do your best, Jake. I'm sure they'll give you a participation ribbon no matter how many questions you answer incorrectly."

Well, thought Jake, *that part of the plan sure worked. She thinks I'm a total idiot.*

"Who are we up against in the first round?" asked Grace.

"Eastside," said Mrs. Malvolio. "I hear they're quite good. Not Sunny Brook good, but good. Oh, there's my uncle Heath. His son Hubert is the captain for Sunny Brook. Excuse me, kiddos. I should go say hello. . . ."

She waltzed away, her chunky necklace clanking as she waved up at the district superintendent, who sort of half waved back.

"She only baked for us because she thinks we're going to lose," said Jake. "She's going to be very disappointed."

Grace chomped a big bite out of a brownie.

"Nerves," she mumbled with her mouth full of gooey chocolate.

"Relax," said Kojo. "We're gonna be great. Because *you're* gonna be great."

"Um-hmmm," said Grace, taking two even bigger bites of brownie.

"There's Hubert Huxley," said Jake as they made their way to their assigned seats in the first row of the bleachers.

"He's the one who came into the cafeteria to invite me to transfer to Sunny Brook," said Grace. "Coincidence? I think not. It was all probably part of their plan."

"And check it out," moaned Kojo. "We have to sit next to the big doofus."

"I'll take that seat," said Jake. "You guys grab the other two."

Jake sat down beside Hubert.

"Ah," said Hubert. "If it isn't the genius who thinks vapid video games about intergalactic zombies are twenty-first-century learning tools."

Jake just nodded. Hubert leaned in closer.

"When this is over, the whole audience will be chanting 'Riverview stinks!' We're going to trounce you. *If* you make it to the finals, that is."

Jake smiled. "Okay."

Hubert laughed. "You ignoramus. 'Trounce' means 'to defeat heavily in a contest.'"

It also means "to rebuke or punish severely," Jake thought. But he didn't say it.

He was still playing dumb.

And Grace was still nervously nibbling brownies.

33

Jake thought the shocked look on Hubert Huxley's face was priceless.

Not to mention the look of shock and horror on Mrs. Malvolio's mug.

Riverview—with Grace, Kojo, and Jake taking turns fielding questions—had breezed through its first two rounds without a single wrong answer.

"You're amazing!" Jake's mom shouted when he answered "A stamp" for the question "In philately, what is an Inverted Jenny?"

They made it to the finals against Sunny Brook Middle School.

During the short break before the final round, Grace's stomach started gurgling. Loudly.

"Are you okay?" asked Jake.

"I think I ate too many brownies," Grace moaned,

clutching her belly. Jake heard a very loud burble, like bubbles in a bathtub. Grace's eyes went wide.

"What's going on, Grace?" asked Kojo. "Do you have aliens in your intestines?"

"I need to go to the bathroom."

"Okay, ladies and gentlemen," chirped the TV meteorologist, Max Myer, who was really enjoying his stint as a game show host. "It's time to start the final round!"

"But I need to go to the bathroom!" Grace whispered through her teeth. "Now!"

"Go ahead, kiddo," Myer said out of the corner of his mouth. "You can rejoin your team when you're finished. But I can't wait. I need to be back in the studio in time to prep for the ten p.m. newscast. There's a cold front moving in."

"Go on," said Jake. "We'll do the best we can without you."

Now Grace was hugging her abdomen with both arms. "I think there was something in those brownies Mrs. Malvolio gave me."

Of course, thought Jake. *Mrs. Malvolio tried to sabotage her own school's chances by taking Grace out of the game. Did she bake a chocolate-flavored laxative into those brownies? Of course she did! It's a classic prank!*

Grace ran out of the gym and into the girls' locker room.

Jake and Kojo sat down at their table to face off against Heath Huxley and his two teammates from Sunny Brook Middle. They were all wearing matching blazers and ties.

"You kids ready?" asked Mr. Myer.

"I was born ready," said Hubert.

"And it's been downhill ever since," cracked Jake.

The audience laughed, and Jake realized he could still be his funny, breezy self. Being smart didn't mean he had to be boring. He'd heard that Albert Einstein was funny.

"Okay," said the quizmaster, "the first question is for Sunny Brook. And since this is the final round, the degree of difficulty has gone up."

"No worries," said Hubert.

Jake's armpits started pumping out sweat. They'd made it to the finals. But now they didn't have Grace. What if he blew it? What if *this* was when the jelly beans wore off?

"For ten points, Sunny Brook, what constellation has an asterism made up of Alnitak, Alnilam, and Mintaka?"

"What's an asterism?" someone shouted from the bleachers.

Hubert grabbed the microphone before either of his two teammates could answer, even though one had her mouth open and was ready to speak.

"Orion!" he shouted.

"Well done. Ten points."

"And," Hubert continued, "for the dimwit in the audience, an asterism is a prominent pattern or group of stars."

Jake rolled his eyes. Hubert might be a genius, but he was also a jerk.

"Oh-kay," said the jolly meteorologist. "Good to know. I guess. Riverview? Here's your ten-point question."

"Bring it on, baby," said Kojo.

"What artist wrote these words: 'When I leave here on this earth, did I take more than I gave?' "

Jake could see the answer floating behind his eyes. It was as clear as the song credits scrolling in a playlist. Jake knew this!

"That would be the American rapper Macklemore, Mr. Myer," said Jake.

"Correct."

The questions flew back and forth. Neither Sunny Brook nor Riverview answered a single question incorrectly. Hubert Huxley answered all the questions for Sunny Brook because, basically, he was a ball hog. Jake and Kojo took turns answering for Riverview.

Kojo had always been smart. But Jake was surprised by some of the correct answers that kept tumbling out of his own jelly bean brain.

"Cenozoic Era."

"Rhinoceroses, or, if you want to be fancy, Rhinocerotidae."

"Dwight D. Eisenhower."

He even nailed some pretty dense math problems like, "Find the least common multiple of six, eight, and sixteen."

"The answer is forty-eight."

"Correct."

Jake and Kojo fist-bumped. This was actually fun!

But Hubert Huxley didn't miss a beat, either. With two questions left to go in the round, the score was still tied.

And Grace was still missing!

"Okay, Sunny Brook, here is your second-to-last question," said the host.

"Or, you know, the penultimate one," cracked Jake. All the brainy people in the audience, like Grace's father and the district superintendent, chuckled.

"For fifteen points, the concept that trace evidence is passed from one person to another during contact is known as what?"

"The contact concept!" blurted Hubert.

"Oooh, no. Sorry, that answer is wrong. Riverview? Would you like to answer this one?"

Suddenly, Jake's brain hit its first brick wall. Apparently, none of the jelly beans carried the chemistry he needed for the concept of "trace evidence." *Is it something about tracing paper? Or tracking footprints in the sand? Where the heck is Grace?*

"We'll answer it, Max," said Kojo. "Unless I'm wrong, which you know I'm not, that concept is known as Locard's exchange principle. I learned that by watching every single one of those *CSI* shows."

"Is that your team's final answer?"

Jake nodded. " 'Locard's principle' is our team answer."

"You are correct. You are now in the lead by fifteen points!"

"Oh yeah, baby!" shouted Kojo. This time, he and Jake slapped a high five.

People in the stands started chanting, "Riv-er-view! Riv-er-view!"

Jake's mom was stomping her feet on the risers in total "We Will Rock You" rhythm, leading the thunderous crowd. Haazim Farooqi was stomping along with her.

The Riverview Pirates hadn't won the Quiz Bowl yet, but all the neighborhood kids and all the grown-ups who'd once been neighborhood kids were, for the first time in a long time, cheering for their tired, worn-down, beloved old friend.

The school that once was and always would be *theirs*.

All Jake and Kojo had to do was answer one more question correctly.

34

"This thing isn't over!" sneered Hubert Huxley.

"You should've let me answer," said Norah Nguyen, one of the smartest kids on the Sunny Brook team. "I watch *CSI* shows, too!"

"Who loves ya, baby?" Kojo said with a wink when he heard that. "You want a Tootsie Pop? I've got grape."

Norah crossed her arms over her chest and glared at him.

Max Myer checked his watch. "It's time for the final two questions. These will each be worth thirty points. If Sunny Brook answers incorrectly, they lose. However, if Sunny Brook answers correctly, and Riverview does not, then Sunny Brook retains its title as Quiz Bowl District Champion. If *both* teams get their answers right, then, ladies and gentlemen, we will be crowning a new champ tonight: Riverview!"

The cheers and foot stomping started up again.

Max Myer raised his arms to quiet the crowd.

"Okay, Sunny Brook. Here is your question."

"Excuse me."

Everyone turned to see Grace hobbling across the basketball court. Jake stood up like he wanted to go help her. Grace waved him off.

"I'm better. Did I miss anything?"

The crowd laughed.

"Just the whole game," said Kojo. "But don't worry. We're up fifteen points."

Grace gave a triumphant arm pump. "Yes!"

"Can we kindly return to the game?" demanded Hubert. "Give us our question, Mr. Myer."

"Right you are, Sunny Brook. Here we go: What king defeated the Revolt of the Earls in 1075 and then, a decade later, ordered the composing of the Domesday, or doomsday, Book?"

"Easy," said Hubert. "My hero. William the Conqueror."

"You are correct! You are now in the lead."

"Because I am Hubert the Conqueror!"

Jake rolled his eyes. So did both of Hubert's teammates.

"It all comes down to this," said Max Myer. "One of these two teams will have the honor of moving on to the State Quiz Bowl competition. Okay, Riverview, for thirty points, in the Spanish version of what blockbuster movie did a wise character say, 'Un gran poder conlleva una gran responsabilidad'?"

Jake and Kojo both looked to Grace. They had terrified expressions on their faces.

Grace smiled.

"*Spider-Man*. Uncle Ben says it to Peter Parker."

Grace turned so she could say it to Jake.

"'Con un gran poder viene gran responsabilidad.' Or, in English, 'With great power comes great responsibility.'"

"That is correct!" shouted Max Myer.

"Sí," said Grace. "I know."

35

"Patricia?" said Dr. Rosalia Lopez, the district school superintendent, after she found the Riverview principal in the bleachers. "First of all, congratulations on your victory."

"Thank you, Dr. Lopez."

"But, if I may, why are your hallways filled with trash? Why are your bathrooms such a mess?"

Mrs. Malvolio blinked repeatedly and smiled blankly as her brain scrambled to come up with a suitable answer. She couldn't find one. She had no choice. She had to blurt out the truth.

"I fired the janitor."

"Excuse me?"

"Frankly, Dr. Lopez, I don't think having someone whose sole job is to clean up after the children sends the right sort of signal."

"Interesting theory, Patricia. But please rehire your custodian. Immediately. I, for one, don't enjoy the fragrant aromas of ripe garbage and raw sewage."

"Of course, Dr. Lopez. I'll send a text. He'll be back on the job first thing tomorrow morning."

"Excellent. And, Patricia, I must say I am impressed. Your students are brilliant. Especially that Jake McQuade . . ."

"Yes, Dr. Lopez," Mrs. Malvolio replied, trying her best to sound delighted and cheerful and super-duper proud. Unfortunately, her face was not playing along. She looked like she'd just sucked a sour lemon. "He's something, our Jake. Really something."

People in the crowd started chanting, "Jake! Jake! Jake!" Then "Kojo! Kojo! Kojo!" And "Grace! Grace! Grace!"

Mrs. Malvolio thought she might be ill.

Dr. Lopez shielded her mouth with the side of her hand so she could speak confidentially.

"As you know, Patricia, because of budget cuts, one middle school in our district will need to be shut down at the end of the year. But after your showing tonight, I don't think it will be yours. I can't wait to see how your team fares at the State Quiz Bowl competition!"

"Me neither," said Mrs. Malvolio. She was smiling so hard, her face hurt.

Down on the gym floor, Jake, Kojo, and Grace were

being mobbed by friends, family, and camera crews from the local TV stations.

"If you'll excuse me, Dr. Lopez, I need to go congratulate my students."

"Looks like they're turning into quite the celebrities," said Dr. Lopez. "My, what a marvelous trio of academic ambassadors for the district! Kudos to you, Patricia. Kudos indeed!"

"Yes. Marvelous. Kudos. Woo-hoo. Excuse me."

Mrs. Malvolio made her way down to the hardwood floor and listened to her "academic ambassadors" talk to the press.

"We owe it all to Riverview Middle School," she heard Grace Garcia tell one of the TV reporters.

"Why does the school look so run-down?" asked the reporter.

"Because it is," said Kojo. "I'm not gonna lie to you, people. This place could use a major face-lift. Maybe some new lockers. And a new refrigerator to keep the chocolate milk from curdling."

"Would your viewers like to know the five basic components of the refrigeration cycle?" asked Jake.

The reporter chuckled a very TV-ish chuckle. "Heh, heh, heh. No thank you, Jake."

"The compressor—"

"That's a cut," said the reporter. The camera operator lowered his rig.

"Thanks, kid," he said to Jake. "We got what we need."

"Will this be on the Sleuth channel?" asked Kojo.

"Maybe," said the reporter. "You kids were so amazing, I wouldn't be surprised if media outlets all over America picked up this story."

"That'd be awesome!" said Grace.

Oh joy, thought Mrs. Malvolio. *Now the school and its resident geniuses are going to be on national TV? We're never going to be able to tear this place down!*

The camera crews packed up their gear. Grace, Kojo, and Jake were still shaking hands and hugging all their friends, family, and admirers.

Mrs. Malvolio shoved her way to the front of the line.

"Excuse me. Principal. Coming through."

"Oh, hi, Mrs. Malvolio," said Grace, narrowing her eyes down to angry slits. "Those brownies were . . . different."

"Old family recipe. Surprisingly marvelous performance this evening, kiddos. Very surprising."

"Thank you, Mrs. Malvolio," said Jake.

"Yes, Mr. McQuade. You were the most *surprisingly* marvelous of all."

"The three of us can't wait to move up to the state competition," said Grace.

"Riv-er-view!" chanted Kojo, pumping his fists over his head. "Riv-er-view!"

Before long, everybody in the gymnasium had picked up the chant again.

Well, everybody except Mrs. Malvolio.

She was too busy trying to figure out how to sabotage the three little geniuses before they ruined all of her and Mr. Huxley's plans.

36

So much garbage had piled up in his brief absence, Mr. Schroeder, the school janitor, had to haul it out of the building in giant rolling trash bins.

"It's good to be back on the job!" he said cheerfully to all the teachers and kids who welcomed him.

"You see that handle on the trash bin?" Jake asked when he saw Mr. Schroeder pushing another load up the hallway.

"Yeah?"

"If you were to tilt the barrel backward and hook that handle to the trailer hitch on the electric golf cart you use for outdoor maintenance, I project you could cut your lugging time by fifty-three point nine percent. Maybe more. You also won't strain your back."

"Thanks, Jake!"

After classes, between bells, Grace, Kojo, and Jake signed a ton of autographs.

"You guys?" said Grace. "We should practice for the state competition today during lunch."

"No can do," said Kojo. "Jake and I have an off-campus appointment."

"It's a doctor thing," said Jake. "Well, he's not really a doctor. Not yet, anyhow. But I need to see him."

"Oh-kay," said Grace. "We still on for seeing Papi after school?"

"Totally," said Jake.

"You sure you two don't want me to come with you after school?" said Kojo.

"That's okay. Papi just wanted to have a little chat with Jake."

"Okay," said Kojo. "But I could help your pop fix his fashion mistakes, Grace. I mean, what's up with the turtleneck and tweed look? It's so last millennium."

Grace laughed. "Good luck with your non-doctor doctor's appointment. See you guys later. And, Jake?"

"Yeah?"

"Thanks."

"For what?"

Grace shrugged. "I dunno. Everything?"

Smiling, she practically skipped down the hall.

"So," said Kojo after Grace glided around a corner, "when are you two getting married?"

"We're not getting married, Kojo. Under current law, the minimum age of marriage in this state is eighteen. We're both twelve. Case closed. Do you have your note from your mom and dad?"

"Yeah. I told them I needed to go with you to the doctor because you're afraid of needles and your mother is busy working a luncheon buffet at the hotel."

"Good cover story. Did you call it needle phobia or aichmophobia? Because both terms can be used to describe the extreme fear of medical procedures involving injections."

"I just said you're afraid of needles, baby. Come on. We need to go see Haazim!"

37

Jake and Kojo took an express bus downtown to Warwick College.

They quickly followed the paths that would take them across the campus to Corey Hall and Mr. Farooqi's subbasement chemistry lab.

"I'd love to talk with you and relive the glory of your performance at the Quiz Bowl last evening," Farooqi said when he let them into his lab. "But this is the one afternoon when I have to teach a class. Well, actually, I don't teach it. I monitor the lecture hall while the undergraduate students listen to a televised lesson from a very distinguished professor, whom, of course, I hope to meet someday."

"Sorry," said Jake. "This was the only time we could leave school."

"We just need to ask you a few questions," added

Kojo, trying his best to sound like the detective he hoped to be one day.

"Very well. But my time is limited. I can't be late to class."

"Of course," said Jake. "I think Shakespeare said it best in act two, scene two of his play *The Merry Wives of Windsor:* 'Better three hours too soon than a minute too late.' "

"Huh," said Kojo. "Wonder which jelly bean that little tidbit was hiding in."

Jake kept going. "Shakespeare also wrote: 'I wasted time, and now doth time waste me.' "

Kojo threw up his arms. "Wasting time is what you're doing right now! Come on, Jake. Cut to the chase, baby. My man Haazim needs to go monitor a TV lecture."

"Right. Sorry."

"Now, then," said Farooqi, making a big show of rocking his wrist to check his watch (which Jake could tell needed a new battery since it wasn't anywhere near nine). "What's so urgent?"

"We have another Quiz Bowl competition in two weeks," said Jake. "Two weeks from Wednesday."

"That means we have twelve days," added Kojo. "See? I haven't eaten a single magical jelly bean but—BOOM— I'm doing that kind of math in my head."

"The smartest kids from all over the state will be there," said Jake. "The event takes place in the grand ballroom of the Imperial Marquis Hotel!"

"That's where Dr. Blackbridge was speaking," said Farooqi.

"It's also where my mother works. And she's been so proud of the smarter version of me. . . ."

"You shouldn't worry, Jake," said Farooqi. "You did quite well last night. I feel certain you'll do equally as well in this next competition."

"But," said Jake, "what if it wears off?"

"I beg your pardon?"

"You said the jelly beans might wear off!"

"I did?"

"Yes! How long do the effects of your Ingestible Knowledge capsules last?"

"How should I know? You're Subject One, remember? That means there haven't been any other subjects. No other research. We're flying blind here, Jake. Coming in on a wing and a prayer. It's touch and go."

"Mr. Farooqi?" said Kojo. "If you ever open an airline, remind me not to fly on it."

"You might stay smart forever, Jake," said Farooqi. "Or it might all disappear tomorrow."

"Why tomorrow?" said Kojo. "Tomorrow's Saturday. Does being smart take the weekend off?"

"I was just making a hypothetical statement," said Farooqi. "Now if you'll excuse me, I'm needed in Bumgartner Hall. My TV lecture class. Those students aren't going to monitor themselves. That would be bedlam. Chaos . . ."

"Are you making more jelly beans?" asked Jake, a hint of desperation in his voice.

"Yes. I'm still working on the Spanish-language formulation. Tweaking the protein mix."

"Can you make more like the ones you made before?"

"Maybe. I don't know. I'm under pressure, too, Jake. I have to document my research. Then I have to write a very long paper about all that research—with footnotes! I also need to do my laundry. I'm almost out of underpants. And on top of all that, I have expenses, Jake. Yes, this is my dream, but biochemical breakthroughs like the ones I'm attempting don't come cheap. And I don't have any research grants or—"

Jake nodded and held up his hand. "We get it. We understand."

"We do?" said Kojo.

"Yes. Miracles can't be rushed."

38

After school, Grace took Jake to visit her dad at Warwick College, where he was the dean of the Education Department.

It was the same college where Haazim Farooqi was a research assistant. But the building where Professor Garcia worked was way nicer.

"He's finishing up a meeting, Grace," said his secretary, "but you can wait in his office."

"Thanks."

"By the way, I saw you kids on the news. You're both brilliant!"

"Gracias!"

Grace and Jake entered Professor Garcia's cluttered office. Grace pointed to one of the dozens of framed photographs decorating the bookcases crowded with books.

"You see that young woman in the picture with Papi?

You met her at the Quiz Bowl. That's District Superintendent Rosalia Lopez back when she was just, you know, Rosie Lopez, college student."

"Another fine product of Riverview Middle School," said Professor Garcia as he strode into the office. "Just like you two. Great to see you again, Jake."

Professor Garcia was wearing another turtleneck sweater under a different tweed blazer. His handshake was very vigorous and made Jake feel like a water pump— the variety known as the suction-and-lift hand pump.

Jake, of course, knew that Dr. Garcia, who had emigrated from Cuba, had received a PhD in Latin American literature with an Afro-Hispanic emphasis. He also liked to sing and cook. His favorite dish to prepare was ropa vieja, often considered the national dish of Cuba.

Jake didn't learn all that from the jelly beans. He'd actually read it in a newspaper article Grace had forwarded to his phone on the bus ride down to the campus.

"A lot of brilliant thinkers have come out of Riverview," the professor said as he gestured for Grace and Jake to sit down. "But, Mr. McQuade?"

"Yes, sir, Professor Garcia?"

"You might be the single most brilliant mind to ever attend the school—at least since my daughter got there."

Grace blushed. "Papi?"

"I'm serious. For decades, Riverview has produced great thinkers, athletes, performers, and business leaders. It's proof of the power of public education. It's why my wife and I insisted that Grace go there. But I must admit, it's a shame that your beloved alma mater has become such a shambles."

Jake had a slightly distressed look on his face. Because, for the first time in his life, he realized that, in Latin, *alma mater* meant "generous or nourishing mother." That was just weird. Who'd call their mother, especially if she was generous and nourishing, a middle school? It'd be rude.

"Jake?" said Dr. Garcia. "Are you still with us, son?"

"Sorry, sir."

"Jake's a little overwhelmed by his recent burst of intelligence," explained Grace. "He had a mental growth spurt."

Jake nodded. "I sometimes surprise myself with the things I suddenly know."

"You seemed to surprise your principal, as well," Professor Garcia said with a chuckle. "I watched Mrs. Malvolio last night. Her mouth was hanging open the whole time you fielded all those questions. Can I be honest with you, Jake?"

"Yes, sir. 'Honesty is the first chapter in the book of wisdom,' according to Thomas Jefferson, who sold all of *his* books to the United States of America after the British burned the original Library of Congress to the ground in 1814."

"Jake?" said Grace. "Focus."

"Right. Thanks."

Professor Garcia chuckled some more. "I like you,

Jake. I like you a lot. But I don't like what Mrs. Malvolio has done to your school."

"Me neither," said Jake. "But what can we do to stop Mrs. Malvolio from tearing it down?"

That seemed to startle Professor Garcia. "Is that her intention?"

"We think so," said Grace. "Her uncle is Heath Huxley. The real estate developer."

"Ah, yes. The notorious Mr. Huxley. He's the one who tore down a senior citizen housing complex to build a shiny mall full of ridiculously expensive shops."

"Mr. Huxley wants to build a high-rise condo right where the school is and call it Riverview Tower," said Jake. "He's already selling apartments in it."

Professor Garcia nodded thoughtfully. "Well, Jake, however you acquired this 'instant intelligence,' it seems you have been given a great gift. If more people learn about your incredible brainpower, you could show this city—nay, this whole country—the power of public education and why we need to keep Riverview Middle doing what it's done for decades!"

As the professor went on to list a lot of incredibly successful people who went to public schools—Oprah Winfrey, Steve Jobs, Ruth Bader Ginsburg, Warren Buffett, and on and on—Jake started to worry that maybe he wasn't cut out for this.

At first, it'd been kind of fun being super smart. A game. Now the future of Riverview Middle School was suddenly riding on his shoulders. And all those brainy public-school people Professor Garcia just mentioned? None of them got their smarts from jelly beans. He was pretty sure theirs mostly came from books, hard work, and old-fashioned studying.

"I'd like to run a few 'intelligence' tests on you, Jake," said Professor Garcia. "Generate some irrefutable proof. Tomorrow's Saturday. Are you free at, say, eleven?"

"Sure." Jake was trying to sound confident.

But inside he was terrified.

39

Early the next morning, Jake rode with Grace and her father back to Warwick College.

"It's the weekend," said Professor Garcia. "We'll have the campus all to ourselves. I hope you don't mind, but I've asked a few of my colleagues to join us as we test your IQ."

"A number designed to rank my intelligence in relation to the entire human population," said Jake.

"That's right. I, of course, think intelligence is much more than a number. And numbers can never give us the full measure of a person. But, well, people like numbers. Numbers give them something they can relate to."

Jake nodded. "Did you know that the abbreviation 'IQ' was coined in 1912 by the psychologist William Stern for the German term 'Intelligenzquotient'?"

"You speak German quite well," remarked Professor Garcia.

"Vielen Dank, Doktor Garcia. It's Spanish I have trouble with."

"I heard that Albert Einstein's IQ was somewhere between one hundred sixty and a hundred ninety!" said Grace.

"Putting him in the 'exceptionally gifted' category," said Professor Garcia.

"What's the highest IQ ever scored, Papi?" asked Grace.

"It's hard to say. Some claim it's Adragon De Mello, who graduated from college at age eleven and supposedly scored a four hundred on his IQ test. But that was never properly certified. We estimate that the IQ for the smartest person on the planet would be approximately one hundred and ninety-four point six."

"Approximately?" Grace said with a laugh.

Her father laughed back. "Approximately."

"Thank you, once again, for agreeing to do this, Jake," said Professor Garcia as he led the way into a lecture hall with at least two hundred seats.

A desk and a chair were set up on the floor at the base of the steep amphitheater. Three adults sat in the front row looking extremely brainy. Grace grabbed a seat in the row behind them.

"Jake," said Professor Garcia, "I'd like you to meet my colleagues. "Doctors Amanda Jones, Milton Thomas, and Jennifer Sniadecki. They do research and lecture in the Education and Psychology Departments."

"Uh, hi," said Jake, giving the three professors a nervous finger-wiggle wave.

They nodded grimly, their faces masks of seriousness.

"They will certify the results of this test before we make them public," said Dr. Garcia.

"We're going to make my score public?"

"Yes. With your permission, of course. It might help sway attitudes about the power of a free public education."

Jake nodded because he remembered his mission and that line from *Spider-Man* about great power and great responsibility. He also remembered that Grace was the one who told it to him.

She gave him a big thumbs-up from the second row.

"Let's do this thing," he said.

"Very well. Let's begin."

Dr. Garcia held up the first card from two tall stacks piled at the edge of the desk.

"What number should come next in this series?" he asked.

1—1—2—3—5—8—13

"Twenty-one," said Jake without missing a beat. "Each number is the sum of the two numbers before it. Thirteen plus eight equals twenty-one."

"Correct," said Dr. Garcia. The professors behind him scribbled on their clipboards.

"Please complete this comparison," said Dr. Garcia, holding up another card.

PEACH is to HCAEP as 46251 is to:

"One five two six four—the numbers in reverse," said Jake.

"Correct." Dr. Garcia held up card number three.

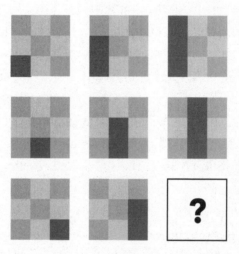

"Please pick the next image in the sequence: A, B, C, D, E, or F."

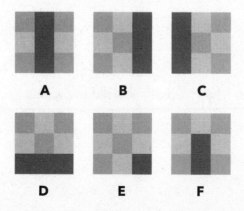

"The answer is 'B,'" said Jake. "The blocks build into a column and then we shift over one space to repeat the same sequence."

"Correct."

And on and on it went. It was easy-peasy all the way.

In the second hour, the trio of professors stopped taking notes and just gawked at Jake as he fired off one correct answer after another. (Luckily, there was no Spanish-language section.)

Later, in the afternoon, after the professors had huddled and made several phone calls, the college held a press conference. Dr. Garcia and his three colleagues boldly proclaimed that "Jake McQuade, according to our certified and documented testing, has an IQ well in excess of three hundred. He is, without a doubt, the smartest kid in the universe!"

Cameras flashed. News crews pushed in for a close-up. Jake had two dozen microphones jabbed into his face.

"And," he said, as heroically as he could under pressure, "I owe it all to Riverview Middle School! The best middle school in the city, maybe the world! Gooooo, Pirates!"

Behind the crowd of eager reporters, Jake could see Grace smiling at him.

She even put her hands together to form a heart.

That's when he really started to sweat.

40

Heath Huxley invited his niece to join him at his pent-house apartment bright and early Sunday morning.

"Are we doing brunch?" Mrs. Malvolio asked with a nervous giggle that made her chunky necklace clatter.

"No. We're watching your student, Jake McQuade, on TV. He's doing *CBS Sunday Morning.* That's the show all the smart people watch when they should be sleeping!"

"What's Jake doing on TV?"

"Didn't you see the news yesterday? Some eggheads at Warwick College certified him as a genius with an IQ that's off the charts!"

Mr. Huxley and Mrs. Malvolio settled into a twin set of plump white chairs in front of the TV.

Mrs. Malvolio looked around the living room. "Do we have snacks?"

"Shhhh! Here he is."

"So, Jake, you're twelve?" asked the interviewer.

"Yes. I'm a seventh grader at Riverview Middle School—that's a public school, a school maintained at public expense, so I want to say thanks to the public."

"He's doing an ad for keeping your wretched school open!" fumed Mr. Huxley. "We have to put a stop to this, Patricia. We have to stop it immediately!"

"Yes, Uncle Heath." She fanned the foul air underneath her nose. When her uncle fumed, he literally exhaled fumes. It was almost as if he had chunks of rotting egg salad sandwiched between his teeth.

"Are you looking forward to the State Quiz Bowl competition?" asked the interviewer.

"Oh yes," replied Jake.

"That's, what, ten days away?"

"Good math," Jake said with a wink.

The reporter chuckled.

"And he's charming, too?" seethed Mr. Huxley. "We need to hatch a plan. We must destroy this boy."

Mrs. Malvolio fanned faster. Her uncle's seething smelled worse than his fuming.

"What are you studying to prep for the competition?" asked the TV interviewer.

Jake shrugged. "Nothing special really. Just what they teach us at Riverview Middle School. Did I mention how awesome it is?"

"Several times. So, Jake, some viewers have sent in questions that they think will stump you. Are you game?"

"Sure. Fire away."

"Okay. This is from Jenna Bellish in Warren, New Jersey."

Jake waved at the camera. "Hey there, Jenna."

"Here's your question: If you take one letter away from the word 'friend' and put the rest into a different order, what word would you create? 'Blend,' 'diner,' 'fiend,' or 'freak'?"

"Ah," said Jake. "Very tricky, Jenna. The answer, of course, is 'diner.' 'Fiend' is the word you would get if you took away one letter—'r' in this instance—but *didn't* rearrange the letters. 'Diner' fulfills both criteria specified in the question."

"You are correct!"

"Shut it off!" demanded Mr. Huxley.

Mrs. Malvolio found the remote and snapped off the TV.

"I'm not going to let that boy stand between me and what is rightfully mine!"

"You mean the buried treasure?"

"Exactly!"

"Well, Uncle Heath, not to be a Debbie Downer, but technically, until we recover the treasure, it's not really"— she made air quotes—" 'rightfully yours.' "

"Oh yes it is, Patricia. It is *my* inheritance. It is *our* family's legacy! Whatever is buried under that school is Mieras money!"

"Excuse me?"

"Our ancient ancestor was Alonso Mieras, a bold seafaring man."

Mrs. Malvolio smiled and nodded as if she understood what the heck Mr. Huxley was talking about, even though she didn't.

"My grandfather, your great-grandfather, was Miguel Mieras. He changed our family name to Huxley because he wanted people to think we were British. That we came from a noble line of dukes and earls, instead of being the direct descendants of a Spanish pirate! One whose treasure was stolen from him by a bratty little cabin boy!"

"Wait a second," said Mrs. Malvolio. "Are you telling me that our ancestor Alonso Mieras was the pirate captain known as Aliento de Perro?"

"Yes!" cried Mr. Huxley. "He was Dog Breath!"

Well, that would certainly explain a lot, thought Mrs. Malvolio.

Mr. Huxley stood up, clutched his hands behind his back, and started pacing around the room.

"For centuries, our family has tried to find the treasure that was stolen from us. My father failed. *His* father failed. And all the fathers before them? Failures!"

"Why didn't someone tell me?"

"Because they didn't want word of their bungling to spread. I was the first to even have an inkling as to where the vile cabin boy had hidden what is rightfully ours— because I paid good money for that information. Now it is up to us to avenge our family's honor and reclaim Dog

Breath's buried treasure. It is our destiny, Patricia. And to fulfill it, we must tear down that school! ¿Me ayudarás en mi búsqueda?"

"Of course I will help you in your quest, Uncle Heath. What do you need me to do?"

"Don't let foolish children crush our dreams. Deal with Jake McQuade, Kojo Shelton, and that brainy girl, Grace Garcia. If she is really related to Mr. Charley Lyons—"

"Oh, she is!"

"Then she is also related to that ungrateful scoundrel and thieving cabin boy, Eduardo Leones!"

"No!"

"Yes! You must do this for our family's honor! Can you? Will you?"

Mrs. Malvolio smiled. "¡Sí, tío! ¡Sí, sí, sí, sí, sí!"

41

Monday morning, the phone wouldn't stop ringing at Jake's apartment.

Fortunately, Kojo had come over to "strategize" with Jake before they headed off to school. Jake's mother was already at work.

"That publicity stunt at the college?" said Kojo, crunching into a piece of cinnamon toast. "Now, *that* was pure genius, baby. You're going to be getting offers to endorse products. I'm thinking Cracker Jacks could be renamed Cracker Jakes!"

"Jake could become an Instagram influencer!" said Emma. "You do know big corporations pay people to promote stuff on social media, right?"

"Of course," said Jake, even though he actually didn't, because stuff like that wasn't included in Mr. Farooqi's jelly beans.

What other information am I missing? he wondered.

"I'm also figuring we can swing a deal with Frito-Lay," said Kojo. "They make Smartfood—that popcorn with the white cheddar cheese you have to scrape off your fingers with your teeth. We post a few snaps of you munching popcorn while doing some kind of Einstein-looking formula at the whiteboard. KA-CHING! Then there's Smartwater. KA-CHING! When you turn sixteen, we talk to the folks who make Smart cars."

Most of the phone calls were from the media. After his ratings-shattering appearance on *CBS Sunday Morning*, everybody wanted Jake on their morning, afternoon, evening, and late-night shows.

Big companies and multinational corporations were calling, too. His mom had a stack of phone messages they'd "look at later—when things settle down." It seemed like everybody in the world wanted the "Smartest Kid in the Universe." (Whenever Jake was shown on TV, that was the caption zipping under him.)

Some callers offered him high-paying consulting positions.

"Maybe this summer," Jake told them. "Mom always says I should look for a summer job, even though I'm too young to get a work permit. I think she was thinking camp counselor, not chief financial officer, but maybe we can work something out. Later. I'm kind of busy right now. We have to save our middle school."

Before the jelly beans wear off, he thought but didn't say.

Yes, he was still worried.

What if his incredibly high IQ vanished as quickly as it had appeared? What if Haazim Farooqi's brain boosters had an expiration date?

"We need to focus on the State Quiz Bowl competition!" Grace told Jake when he and Kojo finally arrived at school.

So on Monday and Tuesday, Mr. Lyons drilled Jake, Grace, and Kojo. He had agreed to be their official Quiz Bowl coach because he really didn't want anybody tearing down the school, either.

"Okay, team—these are some Quiz Bowl questions I found online," he told them. "They'll give us an idea of what you're in for. For instance: What is the largest two-digit prime number less than a hundred?"

"Ninety-seven," Grace, Kojo, and Jake all said at the exact same second.

"Correct," said Mr. Lyons.

On Wednesday, after drilling their way through two dozen questions, they heard a very strange thumping coming from outside the window. It grew louder and louder.

"We should keep going," said Mr. Lyons, raising his voice to be heard over the noise. "We only have one week left to prepare."

The *whump-whump-whump*s outside became more intense. Windows rattled.

"In animal coloring and camouflage," Mr. Lyons

practically yelled, "what characteristic is usually indicated by bright, vivid colors?"

"Poisonous," said Jake.

"Deadly," said Grace.

"Venomous," added Kojo.

Just then, Mrs. Malvolio stepped into the room. She wore bright, vivid colors and an enormous beaded necklace.

"Mr. McQuade?" she screamed over the whapping.

"Yes?" Jake screamed back.

"They tell me you're needed in Washington. The Pentagon."

"What?"

"The Pentagon! Big building? Lots of generals?"

Jake turned to Kojo and Grace. They looked as shocked as he felt.

"There has to be some kind of mistake," Jake said to Mrs. Malvolio. "I'm only twelve. I can't even vote yet."

"Apparently, the United States military doesn't care!" Mrs. Malvolio gestured toward the window, where dust and debris were swirling around in circles. "That's your helicopter. It just landed on our baseball field."

42

Two helmeted Marines burst into the classroom.

They were both wearing tan flight suits and helmets with tinted visors.

"Mr. Jake McQuade?" barked one.

Jake's armpits were working overtime again. Had he done something wrong? Did the United States government know about the jelly beans? Were they after Haazim Farooqi, too?

"Yes, ma'am?"

"Your country needs you, son," said the other. "Please come with us."

"Now?"

"Roger that."

"Right now, son!" hollered the first Marine. She might've been a drill sergeant.

"Um, okay."

"I'm his manager," said Kojo, stepping forward. "Wherever Jake goes, I go, too, baby."

"Fine. We don't have time to argue. We need to be Oscar Mike."

"Huh?" said Mrs. Malvolio with a confused flutter of eyelashes.

"Oscar Mike, ma'am. On the move! We've alerted your mother as to your whereabouts, Mr. McQuade."

"Did she say it was okay?"

"Roger that. We hope to shuttle you back home before midnight."

"Good," said Kojo. "Because it *is* a school night."

"Kojo—I'll let your mom know you won't be home for supper," said Grace.

"Thanks!" said Kojo. He turned to the Marines. "You guys have food on the chopper? Chips or something? Maybe some of those crispy Biscoff cookies I had on an airplane once?"

"Gunny?" said the other Marine, turning his wrist to consult his watch. "General Coleman is waiting for us. We needed to be in DC fifteen minutes ago."

"Let's move, gentlemen."

The two Marines hustled Jake and Kojo out of the school to the waiting chopper.

"This is so cool, dude!" said Kojo as the helicopter lifted off. "I can see my house!"

It took nearly an hour for the high-speed whirlybird to make it to Washington.

"Okay," said Kojo, peering out a window at all the glistening monuments and buildings below. "This is way better than our fourth-grade class trip to DC."

"Did you know that the Washington Monument is five hundred and fifty-five feet tall and was completed in 1884?"

"Yeah," said Kojo. "It was in the brochure."

Soon they were landing at a helipad behind the Pentagon.

"You know why they call it the Pentagon?" Kojo said to Jake as they dashed up the concrete pathway leading to the building with their Marine escort.

"Because it is a five-sided structure," said Jake.

"Correct. Just because we're on some kind of major mission to save America doesn't mean we can't keep prepping for the Quiz Bowl, baby!"

43

Jake and Kojo were whisked through security.

They surrendered their phones and were given laminated high-security clearance badges on lanyards.

"Can I keep this as a souvenir?" Kojo asked. The grim guard didn't answer. She just shook her head. "Okay. That's cool. We're cool. . . ."

"Follow me," said another soldier. He was wearing a helmet. Indoors.

The soldier escorted Jake and Kojo to the National Military Command Center, what some called the War Room.

"This is just like in that *Transformers* movie!" said Kojo, admiring all the giant-screen TVs, glowing maps, and computer terminals.

"This McQuade?" asked a gruff guard.

"Roger that," said the lead Marine.

"Who's the other kid?"

"I'm Kojo Shelton, sir," said Kojo. "I'm kind of like Jake's sidekick. He's Batman, I'm Robin. He's Captain America, I'm Bucky Barnes. He's—"

"We got it," said the guard. "This way."

The guard took Jake and Kojo into a conference room where a gray-haired general with a colorful salad of ribbons on his chest was impatiently waiting for the dozen assorted military personnel seated at the table and clacking their laptops to tell him something he needed to know.

"General Coleman?" said the guard. "We have McQuade."

"About time," grunted the general. "Who's the other kid?"

"Kojo Shelton, sir," said Kojo with a salute. "Sidekick. Reporting for duty."

The general peered at Jake. Sized him up.

"Son, I'm General Joe Coleman. They tell me you're smarter than Einstein."

"I don't know about that, sir," Jake answered modestly. "I did score pretty high on an IQ test."

"This is no time for modesty, son."

"No, sir. Sorry, sir."

The general snatched up a sheet of paper near one of the keyboard clackers.

"We intercepted this coded message from a hostile ship patrolling near the Strait of Hormuz."

Jake nodded. "The only sea passage from the Persian

Gulf to the Gulf of Oman and then out to sea. Twenty-one percent of the world's oil travels through the narrow passage."

"Exactly," said General Coleman, squinting hard. "So, son, can you decode this thing? So far, our top cryptographers, all of whom are assembled here, haven't been able to. What are the hostiles' intentions? Do I need to alert the president and ask him to authorize a preemptive military strike?"

"This is just like that movie," Kojo whispered to Jake.

"What movie?" Jake whispered back.

"The one with the president and the missiles and stuff."

"Mr. McQuade?" said General Coleman. "We need your assistance. And your undivided attention. If we hit them, they will, undoubtedly, hit back."

Okay, now the pressure was really on. *This isn't a Quiz Bowl. This is about missiles and bombs and blowing things up. Lives are at stake! This incident could spark a third world war!*

Jake studied the coded message. "Huh. It kind of reminds me of the codes etched into the *Kryptos* sculpture located on the grounds of the CIA's headquarters in Langley, Virginia."

All the cryptographers in the room stopped tapping their laptop keys so they could hear what Jake had to say. A few of them nodded when he mentioned the sculpture.

"As you probably know, *Kryptos* has four hidden

messages encoded on it. Three have been solved. The fourth hasn't. This message you intercepted seems to be mimicking the ciphertext of that fourth riddle, but with letters from the Persian alphabet, not the twenty-six of our Latin alphabet."

"What's it say, son?"

Jake started blushing. "It's a love poem, sir."

"Come again?"

"It's a Persian love poem. 'This flame of love set my heart on fire. This flood of love drowned me.' Junk like that."

The general scowled at Jake. "You're telling me it's a la-di-da love letter?"

"Yes, sir. I think somebody on the boat is lonely. He and his girlfriend back home are probably totally into secret codes and junk."

The general's scowl melted into a smile. Then he started laughing. Big, hearty, room-rumbling laughs.

Pretty soon, all the code crackers in the room were laughing and applauding, giving Jake a standing ovation.

"Well done, son," said the general. "You just saved us from making a major military blunder. Well done, indeed!"

"Thanks. Well, we should probably chopper back home now. It's kind of late. . . ."

"And," said Kojo, "as you may know, General Joe, it *is* a school night."

44

"Thank you for your service," General Coleman said to Jake, giving him a hearty salute.

Then he turned to Kojo. "You too, sidekick."

"Thank you, sir," said Kojo. "Our honor, sir."

A military aide entered the room. He was holding Jake's cell phone.

"Sorry to interrupt," said the aide. "Mr. McQuade has been receiving a series of urgent texts."

"Give him his phone," commanded the general. "This boy just saved our butts."

Jake wondered who had been texting. Probably his mom. Or Grace. Maybe Mr. Lyons. Maybe all of them!

The instant Jake touched the phone, it started thrumming.

He glanced at the caller ID: HAAZIM FAROOQI.

"Excuse me, sir," Jake said to the happy general. "I need to take this. It's kind of urgent. And private."

The general nodded toward a side room.

"Thanks. Wait for me here, Kojo."

"Roger that," said Kojo, because all the military people said it a lot.

Jake stepped into the side room.

"Hello?" he said into the phone. "This is Subject One."

"Jake? It's me. Haazim!"

"I know. Your name popped up on the screen."

"Oh. Then why didn't you say, 'Hello, Haazim,' or 'Wazzup, Haazim,' or—"

"Because you always call me Subject One!"

"I do? I don't recall doing that. . . ."

"It doesn't matter. What's this about? I'm kind of busy."

"Oh, *you're* busy? What about me? Doing research. Boiling ramen noodles. Tinkering with my Ingestible Knowledge formulas."

"Or formulae."

"Right. Those. So, Subject One, this is my urgent status report. I may have an antidote. I may also have a Spanish-language jelly bean. Which one do you want me to complete first?"

Okay, this was a new conundrum (what old Jake would've just called a difficult question). If there was an antidote, should Jake take it? What if his country needed him to prevent some other armed conflict? But if he took an antidote, he could go back to just being easy-breezy Jake. No stress. No one counting on him. Nothing to worry about except where his next slice of pizza might be coming from and how to make it to the next level of *Revenge of the Brain Dead*.

"Um, can you work on both?"

"Sure, sure," Farooqi said sarcastically. "I'll whip up *two* new jelly beans. No problem."

"Mr. Farooqi?"

"Yes?"

"I really appreciate all that you are doing. I mean, you're the one who actually did the work. I just got hungry. You're the real genius in this thing, not me. This is your big discovery, not mine."

There was silence for a moment.

"Thank you, Subject One. I sincerely appreciate that sentiment. But, Subject One?"

"Yes?"

"Don't tell anybody. I couldn't stand the pressure. I've seen how those vultures descend upon you on TV. That sort of life isn't for me. I don't want anybody knowing about the jelly beans until I'm confident I can replicate what I created the first time."

"But—"

"I insist."

"Okay. Your secret—*our* secret is safe. No one knows except you, me, and Kojo."

"Good. Now, if you'll excuse me, I must return to my laboratory. My purple goop is boiling over a Bunsen burner. So are my ramen noodles."

They clicked off.

Jake stepped back into the War Room.

Kojo was gone. The general and all the cryptographers and other military people were gone.

The only two people in the room were two very muscular figures in dark suits, a man and a woman, both wearing sunglasses (even though they were in a windowless room). They also had bodyguard-style curly-wire earpieces.

"Mr. McQuade?" said the woman.

"Yes, ma'am?"

"Special Agent Sydney Tillman, FBI."

45

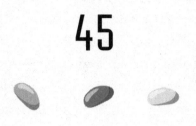

"Oh-kay," said Jake. "Have you seen my friend Kojo? Kojo Shelton? He's my age, wears glasses. . . ."

"The Marines are ferrying him home on a military transport, after a quick stop at Shake Shack for something called a Shack Stack and a concrete." She took a step forward. "The Pentagon advised us you were here in DC, Jake. We could use your assistance."

"Tonight? Because it's a school night. My mother—"

"Was very proud to hear that you would be helping the Federal Bureau of Investigation solve a major case."

"She was?"

The agents nodded.

"She wants you to call her later. She and Emma would both like to hear from you and tell you how proud they are of you. Your mother would also like to remind you to brush your teeth at some point before going to bed."

Jake grinned. He really did like his mom being proud of him on a regular basis. Emma, too.

"We assured your mother that you would be well taken care of during your stay in Washington," Tillman continued. "We've booked you into a child-friendly hotel that will, on request, deliver handmade ice cream sandwiches to your suite. Agent Patrick Andrus, here, will be bunking next door to you for security purposes and to provide transportation to FBI headquarters first thing in the a.m."

"How long will I, uh, be staying here?"

"That depends on how long it takes you to crack the case."

"I have a social studies quiz tomorrow."

"I feel confident this will count as extra credit."

"Oh. Okay. Then let's get to work."

"Not tonight," said Tillman. "Tonight you grab some chow and some sleep. First thing tomorrow Agent Andrus will deliver you to Deputy Assistant Director Don Struchen. And, Mr. McQuade?"

"Yes, ma'am?"

"Your country's counting on you."

Jake ordered room service and scarfed down a fancy cheeseburger and two of those handmade ice cream sandwiches. He also packed up all the little bottles of shampoo and hand lotion and mouthwash in the bathroom. Emma would like those.

He picked up his phone to FaceTime with his mom and Emma and saw a text from Grace:

> You are my superhero! Kojo filled me in. Thanks for saving America.

Grinning, Jake thumbed an app and video-called home.

"Were you really with a general like Kojo told us?" said Emma, her eyes wide with amazement. "Was it the room with all the computers and junk from that movie?"

"Yeah," said Jake. "It was pretty awesome."

"You are so cool, Jake."

"So are you, bro."

"Jake? I'm your sister."

"Jake?" said his mom, sounding kind of choked up. "We're so proud of you. But, honey?"

"Yeah?"

"How are you holding up? This is a lot of pressure. Being on TV. Helping the Pentagon. Working with the FBI. You're still only twelve, hon."

"True," said Jake.

And then he said what he knew his mother wanted to hear because maybe by saying it out loud he could convince himself that it was true.

"I'm fine, Mom. Trust me. It's like Shakespeare said: 'Be not afraid of greatness. Some are born great, some achieve greatness, and some have greatness thrust upon them.' Guess I'm just in the thrust-upon category."

"Um, okay, honey. But you know we think you've always been great."

"Even when you were lazy," added Emma.

That made Jake laugh. "Love you guys!"

"Love you back!"

And after ordering one more ice cream sandwich (with sprinkles on top), Jake fell asleep with a smile on his face.

46

The next morning, after a breakfast in bed of pancakes and French toast (with real maple syrup) plus two orders of bacon, while watching ESPN on a jumbo-screen TV, Jake had a quick FaceTime chat with Grace.

"Good morning!" she said.

"Hey. Sorry I'm missing so many Quiz Bowl practices. It's less than a week away."

"That's okay, Jake. You don't really need them as much as Kojo and I do. Besides, Kojo texted me last night while he was flying home on the helicopter. He told me how you guys saved the world. He didn't get into any details, though. . . ."

"They just needed a little help cracking a code. Turns out, I'm pretty good at that. The easiest questions on your father's IQ test were the more visual ones. The puzzles."

"Excellent," said Grace. "Because when you get back, Uncle Charley and I have another code for you to crack."

"Seriously?"

"Yep. It's been in our family for centuries. It's also in Spanish."

"Oh. I, uh, don't speak Spanish."

"So I've heard. And you can't read it, either. Correct?"

"Correct."

"Well, don't worry, Jake. We can work on this secret code together."

"I'd like that."

"Me too," said Grace.

Someone rapped their knuckles on Jake's hotel room door.

"Mr. McQuade?" said the muffled voice of Special Agent Andrus. "It's time to go. Deputy Assistant Director Struchen has assembled the team at the Hoover Building. They're waiting for us."

"Be right with you. Grace? I gotta go."

"Good luck, Jake. Have fun. And use that big brain of yours to help them catch the bad guys!"

Agent Andrus drove Jake in a sleek black sedan to the FBI's flag-draped, no-nonsense, honeycomb-of-concrete headquarters building on Pennsylvania Avenue.

They passed through security (Jake got another pretty cool temporary ID badge) and headed upstairs to a conference room, where a buttoned-up man with a snowy-white crew cut named Deputy Assistant Director Struchen was waiting with half a dozen field agents. Pictures and photographs were pinned to bulletin boards lining the walls.

"Welcome, Mr. McQuade. I'm Don Struchen."

They shook hands.

"Please take a seat."

"Is there assigned seating?"

"No. Just grab any empty chair."

"Um, okay," Jake mumbled as he sat down. "In school, some of the teachers have a chart. . . ."

"Here's our case."

Struchen went to the bulletin boards and tapped photos and drawings with a pointy aluminum stick as he presented the facts.

"Two weeks ago, a bank in Bakersfield, California, was robbed by two men. We suspect this gentleman, Mick Shaffer, a resident of Bakersfield, was one of them. However, on the day of the bank robbery, Mr. Shaffer was visiting his brother, Bob, in Columbus, Ohio. He flew there, rented a car, and didn't fly home until three days after the bank robbery."

Jake raised his hand to ask a question.

"Yes, son?"

"Does this guy's brother own a car?"

Struchen nodded.

"Then why'd he have to rent one? I mean, unless his

brother was too lazy to come pick him up at the airport. I guess that's possible. I used to be super lazy. I might've told Emma to rent a car or grab a cab if, say, there was a good game on TV and I didn't want to go pick her up. But that's beside the point. I can't drive. Not for four more years."

The FBI agents were all staring at Jake, probably wondering why they asked this kid to help them. They didn't know that sometimes, when the pressure was on, Jake McQuade just babbled.

Struchen cleared his throat. "We have impounded the rental vehicle as evidence. Mr. Shaffer put on a lot of mileage."

Jake studied the bulletin boards. Saw a map of the continental United States. Did some quick math.

"Was it over four thousand five hundred and seventeen miles? 'Cause that would be the length of a round trip to Bakersfield from Columbus and back."

Struchen nodded.

"And was he with his brother for more than sixty-six hours? That's how long it would take to do the driving, give or take an hour or two. He might've stopped for gas. Or to use the bathroom. Or grab some chips. Maybe a doughnut."

"Yes," said Struchen. "He was there for a whole week."

"So it's possible that Mr. Shaffer flew to Columbus, drove to Bakersfield, robbed the bank, and drove back to

Ohio, where he caught a flight home to California a few days later to give himself an alibi?"

"That's what we think," said Struchen, planting his hands on the conference table and leaning in. "It's why the Bureau is involved. We think this was an interstate crime."

"Me too," said Jake, wishing Kojo could've stayed for this part of the trip. All these detectives and evidence and pictures pinned to bulletin boards? Kojo would've loved it. Jake wondered if the FBI would let him take pictures. Probably not.

"So tell me," said Struchen, "how do we prove it?"

Jake leaned back in his chair. And thought.

This was a hard one.

A fly flitted through the room. Agent Tillman followed it with her eyes. Then, in a flash, she grabbed it out of the air and squished it.

That reminded Jake of the road trip his mom took them on last summer. To the Grand Canyon. By the time they made it all the way to Arizona, their car's license plate and grill were splattered with bug guts and mangled wings.

"You still have the car?" he asked.

"Yes," said Struchen. "The rental company has been very cooperative."

"Okay. Have your people in Ohio scrape the windshield and the grill. The front license plate, too, if there is one. We need to analyze any and all squished bugs."

"Squished bugs?"

Jake nodded. "You're also going to need an expert entomologist. Someone who can identify all the insects."

The FBI agents scrambled and made phone calls. Jake leaned back in his chair and grinned. It was pretty awesome to have all these grown-ups listening to him. Maybe adults should listen to kids more often!

Four hours later, Jake was presented with the entomologist's lengthy report. He scanned the list.

"Here we go," he announced. "Two species of Hemiptera, or 'true bugs'—*Neacoryphus rubicollis* AND *Piesma brachiale*—plus the leg of a rainbow grasshopper, all of which are endemic to the western United States, not Ohio."

"Brilliant!" said Deputy Assistant Director Struchen. He turned to his agents. "Tell the team in Bakersfield to arrest Mr. Shaffer. Have the field team in Ohio pay a visit to the brother. And let all the lawyers know about our new evidence. Mr. McQuade?"

"Yes, sir?"

"I can't thank you enough."

"My pleasure, sir. And, sir?"

"Yes?"

"If anybody asks, you might tell them that this arrest was made possible, in part, thanks to the fine public education offered at Riverview Middle School."

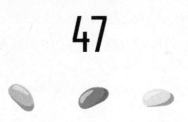

47

Jake received a hero's welcome when he returned to Riverview on Friday morning.

Banners festooned the much cleaner hallways. Kids decorated their lockers with art and copies of the headlines in all the newspapers:

LOCAL GENIUS CRACKS CASE FOR FBI

EGGHEAD SCRAMBLES ROBBERS' ALIBI

JAKE MCQUADE = BRAINIAC^2

Kojo had a stack of T-shirts printed with Jake's class picture and *genius* spelled out using letters from the periodic table of elements.

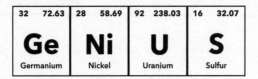

32 72.63	28 58.69	92 238.03	16 32.07
Ge	**Ni**	**U**	**S**
Germanium	Nickel	Uranium	Sulfur

He was selling them at the school supplies shop in the main corridor and proclaimed that all proceeds would be going to the "maintenance and general betterment" of Riverview Middle School.

Jake was back to knocking knuckles with all his buds.

"You're a real inspiration," said Mr. Lyons, shaking Jake's hand.

"No, sir," Jake told him. "*You* are. Even though this building is a wreck, you never gave up on us. You wanted me to learn even when I didn't. You pushed me to be better at b-ball. It's like a quote I read on a coffee mug once."

"What'd it say, Jake?"

"I forget. But I wish I had that mug so I could give it to you right now!"

All the kids hanging in the halls broke into a cheer.

Which was soon cut off by the crackling speakers in the ceiling.

"Students? This is your principal speaking." Mrs. Malvolio's voice echoed off the walls. "You are to report to your homerooms immediately. You will not congregate in the halls for an unauthorized pep rally. You will also remove any and all balloons, banners, and celebratory decorations. Might I remind you that this is a school, not Party City?"

Bummed out by their principal, everybody shuffled off to class. By lunchtime, all the decorations were in the dumpsters.

"Of course Mrs. Malvolio is upset by your achievements," Grace told Jake when they grabbed a table with Kojo in the cafeteria. "She doesn't want us to succeed. If we keep showing the world how smart kids are here, no way is the city shutting down Riverview."

"You up for signing autographs, baby?" asked Kojo.

Jake shook his head. "Not today. We have work to do."

"We sure do," said Grace.

Kojo stood up. "No autographs today, people," he announced. "My man needs a little space. His brain's been working overtime this week."

Everybody nodded. Several were wearing those GENIUS T-shirts.

"By the way, Jake," said Kojo, "while you were down in DC helping the G-men—"

"I so wish you could've been there, Kojo."

"Next time, baby. I was busy up here. Dug a little deeper. Picked up some fresh intel."

"From whom?" said Jake, because that was grammatically correct.

"Mrs. Malvolio herself," said Kojo, gesturing for Jake and Grace to lean in closer. "I was in the office, pretending to admire those pens they have with the plastic flower tops. Anyway, Mrs. Malvolio had her door wide open. She was on the phone with her uncle, Heath Huxley. She's definitely working with him."

"Are you sure?" asked Grace.

"Totally. She said"—Kojo put on a funny, high-pitched

voice and started pretending to fidget with a chunky
necklace—" 'Oh, Uncle Heath, I'd prefer the green carpet in my free penthouse apartment in the new building.
Green will remind me of all the money we're going to
make!' Then, I heard her say something else." Kojo lowered his voice. "I think she knows about that pirate booty
you told us about, Grace."

Grace's eyes went wide. "Why? What'd she say?"

" 'Once the bulldozers get here, Dog Breath will pay
for everything!' "

"They know about the treasure!" said Grace. "We need
to move fast. You guys? We need to go see Uncle Charley."

48

"No more secrets," said Grace when the group was safely inside Mr. Lyons's office, the converted custodian's closet.

"You sure it's okay we're in here?" said Jake.

"It's fine," said Grace. "I texted Uncle Charley. He's on his way. Look, you guys, Uncle Charley and I know something that we haven't shared with anybody. A secret."

Jake and Kojo glanced at each other.

They had a secret, too.

A big one.

A secret about jelly beans and Ingestible Knowledge and an oddball scientist named Haazim Farooqi that they hadn't shared with anybody, either.

But Jake had promised Mr. Farooqi that he wouldn't reveal anything about the IK breakthrough until the scientist was confident he could re-create what he'd done with that first batch of jelly beans.

Plus, Jake wasn't too keen on confessing to Grace (and the world) that he'd more or less cheated his way to his high IQ. That he was a phony and a fraud. That he was only the smartest kid in the universe because, one night, he wolfed down the first sugary snack he could find without exerting any effort.

"Secrets are a bad thing," said Kojo.

"Unless," Jake quickly countered, "revealing them could hurt somebody. For instance, if you knew that someone, say, had created a revolutionary new secret recipe for, I don't know, bubbling purple goop over a Bunsen burner, and they shared that secret with you, it'd be bad to blab about it to anybody."

"True," said Kojo, nodding to confirm he understood what Jake was really saying. "Bubbling purple goop over a Bunsen burner is a whole different, top-secret kind of category."

Grace rattled her head like she was trying to clear Jake's and Kojo's words out of her ears. "What are you two talking about?"

"Nothing," said Jake. "It's just a hypothetical ethics debate."

"About purple goop," added Kojo. "Bubbling. In a beaker . . ."

The door opened. Mr. Lyons quickly slipped into the cramped room, pulling the door shut behind him.

"Have you told them?" he asked Grace.

"I'm trying. Can you two forget about the bubbling

purple goop for a nanosecond? I'm trying to reveal our big family secret!"

"And I need to get back to class," said Mr. Lyons.

"Right," said Jake.

"Go on," added Kojo.

"We need your brainpower, guys," Grace said to Jake and Kojo. "And we need it fast. Uncle Charley?"

"Grace is correct. We need help. My family has tried to do this on our own for centuries. But now that Mrs. Malvolio and her uncle seem to know . . ."

He went to a shelf and pushed aside a cardboard filing box to reveal a small safe. He worked the combination. The heavy steel door sprang open.

"Aha!" said Kojo. "So that's the real reason why our vice principal has his office in an old custodian's closet! Not only does it have a secret doorway to a fallout shelter, but it also comes with a hidden wall safe."

Mr. Lyons reached into the safe and pulled out a document that was sealed inside a thick plastic sheet. It was an antique parchment, the pale brownish color of a tea stain.

"What is that?" asked Kojo.

"This," said Mr. Lyons dramatically, "is the cabin boy Eduardo Leones's treasure map!"

49

Jake studied the sealed document.

It definitely didn't look like a map. More like an antique letter.

"This parchment is very fragile," said Mr. Lyons. "Of course it's also nearly three hundred years old. This was written before the American Revolution."

He pushed away a pile of papers and very carefully laid the protected sheet on his desk.

"Where'd you get it?" asked Jake.

"From my father," said Mr. Lyons. "Who received it from his father. Who received it from his father. And so on, all the way back to 1728."

"How come there's nothing but words?" said Kojo. "Most treasure maps have landmarks and dashes and an 'X' to mark the spot where the treasure's buried. And if it's a pirate map, it should also have a skull and cross-bones on it somewhere."

"This map," explained Grace, "is more like a riddle. A seemingly easy yet remarkably complex puzzle."

"It would be a lot easier if everything down below had remained exactly as it was when young Eduardo wrote it," said Mr. Lyons. "All we know for certain is that the treasure is hidden in a cavernous room underneath this school."

"Is that where your 'fallout shelter' tunnel really leads?" asked Kojo. "Down to the caves?"

"Yes," said Mr. Lyons. "If you follow it beyond the old shelter. The treasure is also why someone from the Leones or Lyons family has stood guard on this land since our ancestor, the extremely clever cabin boy, Eduardo, hid his treasure."

"I've done a lot of research at the library on pirate history in this area," said Grace. "Trying to see if I could fill in some of the blanks."

"Was that the leather-bound journal in the bag that you had at the library?" asked Jake.

Grace nodded. "I was hoping I could find a similar style of 'treasure map,' one that was all words."

"Any luck?" asked Kojo.

Grace shook her head. "Nope."

"Then," said Jake, "it's up to us!"

Kojo snapped several photos of the parchment, holding his phone sideways, like he'd seen spies do in movies.

"You kids don't need me," said Mr. Lyons. "I've tried to figure this thing out for thirty-some years. I'm no good with puzzles. I leave that up to you three."

"We won't let you down, Coach," said Jake. "We're gonna unbury your family's buried treasure!"

50

The three friends spent all day Saturday working with the treasure puzzle in Jake's bedroom.

"Can we crack open the window, baby?" said Kojo. "I'm burning up."

Jake jimmied up the window. "Sorry. Steam heat radiators."

"It's also very hot heat."

Grace had a photo of the treasure puzzle up on Jake's computer monitor. Jake's mom set them up with soda and snacks—including a bag of Pirate's Booty cheese puffs, which made the three friends laugh.

"What?" said Jake's mother. "What's so funny?"

"Nothing," said Jake. "It's just the perfect snack. Cap'n Crunch would be good, too." Then he forced himself not to giggle.

But Grace couldn't help herself. Neither could Kojo.

They both cracked up.

"Emma?" Jake's mom called down the hall. "Maybe you and I should go catch a movie. Let these three work on whatever hysterical project it is they're working on."

"Awesome!" said Emma.

Jake, Grace, and Kojo had the apartment all to themselves. The photo of the ancient parchment glowed on Jake's computer screen:

En esta cueva, encontrarás dos pilares de piedra. Llamémoslos A y B. También encontrarás los restos de mi pozo de fuego. Comienza en el pozo de fuego y cuenta el número de pasos que toma caminar en línea recta hasta el pilar A. Al llegar al pilar, gira noventa grados hacia la izquierda y da el mismo número de pasos. Al llegar, haz una marca en el suelo. Regresa al pozo de fuego y cuenta el número de pasos que toma llegar al pilar B caminando en línea recta. Al llegar al pilar, gira noventa grados hacia la derecha y da el mismo número de pasos. Haz otra marca en el suelo. Escarba en el lugar que está en medio de ambas marcas y ahí, mis hijos, encontrarás mi tesoro.

"Okay," said Grace, "I'll translate the text, line by line."

"Great," said Jake. "And maybe I can, you know, pick up some Spanish along the way."

"Oh-kay. 'En esta cueva, encontrarás dos pilares de piedra.' That means, 'In this cave, you will find two stone pillars.'"

"Those would be the 'dos pilares de piedra,'" said Jake.

"¡Perfecto!" said Grace.

"That means 'perfect-o,'" said Kojo. "Or, you know, 'Oh, perfect!'"

"Let's draw this as we translate it," suggested Jake.

"Good idea," said Kojo, grabbing some graph paper.

"Hang on, you guys," said Grace. "This next part will help us map it out. 'Llamémoslos A y B.' That means, 'Let's call them A and B.'"

"Because," said Jake, "the Spanish words for 'A' and 'B' are 'A' and 'B.'"

"This is starting to resemble a geometry problem," said Kojo, labeling two random points A and B.

"'También encontrarás los restos de mi pozo de fuego,'" Grace continued. "'You will also find the remains of my fire pit.'"

"That's his 'pozo de fuego,'" said Kojo, marking a third random point on the graph paper and labeling it C.

Grace led them through the rest of the translation. Jake and Kojo mapped out all the spots her ancestor from the seventeen hundreds mentioned.

Start at the fire pit and count the number of steps it takes to walk straight to Pillar A. When you reach the pillar, turn ninety degrees to the left and take the same number of steps. When you arrive, make a mark on the ground. Return to the fire pit and count the steps to Pillar B by walking in a straight line. When you reach it, turn ninety degrees to the right and take the same number of steps. Make another marker on the ground. Dig in the place that is halfway between both marks, and there, my children, you will find my treasure!

Jake drew a triumphant *X* to mark the spot halfway between the two markers.

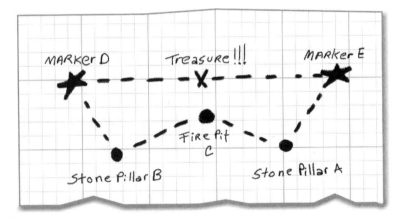

"Boom!" he said. "This will be easy."

"No, it won't," said Grace. "Because Uncle Charley, his father, his grandfather—they've all been down in the cave and found the treasure chamber. They can find the two rock pillars. But the fire pit isn't there anymore!"

"But everything depends on the location of the fire pit," said Kojo.

"Exactly," said Grace. "That's why nobody in my family's been able to find the treasure for close to three hundred years."

Suddenly, someone rang the doorbell. Repeatedly.

"It must be Mom and Emma," said Jake. "They probably forgot their keys. I'll go let them in."

"I need to use the bathroom," said Grace.

"I need some more soda," said Kojo.

"Five-minute break," said Jake. He shut down the computer and hid the graph paper map in the bottom drawer of his desk under a stack of video game cheat guides.

"Paranoid much?" joked Grace.

"It's very valuable information. We should take precautions."

It was a good thing he did.

Because it wasn't Jake's mom ringing the doorbell.

It was Mrs. Malvolio.

51

"Oh, hello, Jake," said Mrs. Malvolio, batting her eyes. "Is your mother home?"

"No," said Jake. "Is there some reason you're here on a weekend, Mrs. Malvolio?"

Grace and Kojo came into the foyer.

"Yeah," said Kojo, plunking a fresh Tootsie Pop into his mouth. "This isn't school."

"This is a private residence!" added Grace.

"Oh, goody." Mrs. Malvolio clapped her fingertips together daintily. "You're *all* here. I brought presents! May I come in?"

Jake reluctantly stepped out of the doorway.

Mrs. Malvolio picked up a festively decorated shopping bag and came inside. She looked around the living room. Her nose crinkled. So did the edges of her forced smile.

"My, oh my. Your apartment is certainly . . . quaint. And cozy!"

"What's in the bag?" asked Kojo.

"Gifts! I hope I guessed your sizes correctly."

She reached into the bag and pulled out three yellow T-shirts with sparkling black letters spelling out BRAINIACS.

"The big day's this Wednesday!" she gushed. "I wanted you to have proper team uniforms for the competition."

"Are those sequins?" asked Kojo. "Because I really don't do sequins. . . ."

"They're lovely," said Grace. "Thanks."

"Yes," said Jake. "Thanks."

Mrs. Malvolio stood there. Smiling. Batting her eyes.

"Could I trouble you for some water? Feeling a mite parched."

"Let me grab you a bottle out of the fridge," said Jake.

As he walked to the kitchen, he tried to figure out the real reason for Mrs. Malvolio's unexpected weekend visit.

Did she know they were working on the cabin boy's treasure puzzle?

How could she?

Unless she had a spy camera set up in the janitor's closet. No. Mr. Lyons would've seen it and taken protective measures. He would've stacked boxes, books, and file folders to block it.

Jake grabbed a small bottle of water out of the fridge

and realized that there were some things even the smartest kid in the universe couldn't figure out. Like what was up with Mrs. Malvolio.

"Here's some water," he said, handing her the chilled bottle.

"Thank you, Jake." She twisted off the cap and guzzled a big gulp. Then she waited, smiled, and batted her eyes some more. After a few seconds, she tilted the bottle to her lips and guzzled again. She twisted the cap back on. Waited. She unscrewed the cap. . . .

"You can take the bottle with you if you want," said Jake. "Just be sure to dispose of it in a recycling bin. Because enough plastic is thrown away each year to circle the Earth four times."

"Oh," said Mrs. Malvolio. "Let's hope there's a question about recycling at the Quiz Bowl!" She glanced at her watch. "Well, this has been fun, but I do need to run." She giggled. "I rhymed! Did you hear that? I'm a poet and didn't know it, although my shoes kind of show it."

"Yes, ma'am." Jake led her to the door and out into the hall. "See you on Monday, Mrs. Malvolio."

She shook a pair of invisible pom-poms. "Go, team!"

Jake came back into the apartment and closed and locked the door.

"Okay," said Kojo. "That was weird. And I am not wearing that spangly T-shirt."

"We'll wear what we wore last time," said Grace as

the team strolled back to Jake's bedroom. "Black polo shirts and Pittsburgh Pirates baseball caps."

"Man," said Kojo as they stepped into Jake's bedroom. "It's burning up in here again."

"Because," said Jake, nodding toward the window, "whoever snuck in here from the fire escape while we were being distracted by Mrs. Malvolio was polite enough to close the window on their way out."

52

Jake checked to make sure nothing was missing from his bedroom.

"They were probably looking for this," he said, retrieving their first draft of the treasure map from its hiding place in the bottom right-hand drawer.

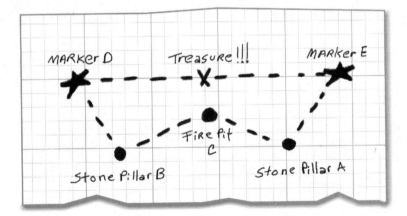

"Or this," said Grace, summoning the photo of the cabin boy's puzzle on Jake's computer. "You guys? We need to start our search for the treasure ASAP. Mrs. Malvolio and her uncle are definitely trying to find it, too."

"But," said Kojo, stroking his chin thoughtfully, "how could they know we know what we know?"

"They must've finally made the connection between Uncle Charley Lyons and the Cubano cabin boy Eduardo Leones. We need to move fast."

"Let me work the puzzle a little longer," said Jake. "Maybe we're not seeing something obvious."

"This is going to be tough without the fire pit," said Kojo.

"But not impossible," said Jake. "It's just a very challenging plane geometry problem. How do we find 'X' without knowing 'A'? I may need to ask an expert for help."

"You gonna call Haazim Farooqi?" said Kojo. "Ask him to whip up a new solution?"

"Who's Haazim Farooqi?" said Grace.

"A, er, geometry expert we know," said Jake swiftly. "He might be able to 'whip up a solution' to this problem."

"You guys know a geometry expert?" said Grace.

"Sort of." Jake's armpits were getting soggy again. He hated even half lying to Grace. But he'd hate her knowing he was a phony genius even more. She wouldn't be making any more heart hands at him if she did.

"But I don't think we'll need his help on this one."

Jake said that last bit directly to Kojo.

He winked to say, *Got it, bro.* Fortunately Grace didn't see him. She was too busy staring at the graph paper map.

"Tomorrow's Sunday," said Grace. "The school will be closed. If Uncle Charley opened it up for us, it might draw more attention to what we're doing. We have to assume that Mrs. Malvolio and Heath Huxley have people monitoring all the security cameras. Work the puzzle, Jake. Try to figure it out. We start our treasure hunt right after school on Monday!"

53

Sunday morning, Jake's mom took him and Emma to the Imperial Marquis Hotel for their world-famous brunch buffet.

"The State Quiz Bowl competition is first thing Wednesday," she said between bites of eggs Benedict. "But we'll start setting up the grand ballroom on Tuesday. They need a pair of giant video screens to project the questions and answers. And they're expecting an audience of over one thousand! Busloads of kids and teachers are coming from all over the state. It's so exciting. I can't wait to see you in action again, hon! Go, Pirates!"

Jake's mom was just one of hundreds of adults who were pulling for Riverview in the championship round because it had been their middle school, too.

"Quick, Jake," said Emma with a grin. "Why are

those called eggs Benedict? Is it because that's what Benedict Arnold used to eat for breakfast?"

"No, Emma," said Jake, returning her grin. "Some give credit for the dish to Pope Benedict the Thirteenth, who was put on a strict eggs and toast diet. However, most culinary experts agree that the dish was named after Lemuel Benedict, a Wall Street stockbroker who wandered into a hotel one morning in 1894 and, hoping to find a cure for his grogginess, ordered buttered toast, poached eggs, crisp bacon, and a dollop of hollandaise sauce. Canadian bacon was soon substituted for the regular bacon, and the rest is, as they say, history."

Emma laughed. "You've still got it! Those other teams don't stand a chance!"

Feeling great, Jake and his happy family returned home.

They were surprised to see a knot of people, many in dark blue police windbreakers, clustered outside their apartment door.

"Is there some problem?" asked Jake's mom, hurrying down the hallway with her keys.

"I'm afraid so," said District Superintendent Lopez, emerging through the wall of police officers. She held up a very official-looking document. "This is a warrant, Ms. McQuade. We need to search your son's bedroom."

54

Jake's mom opened the door for the police and Dr. Lopez.

"What exactly are you looking for?" she demanded.

"The answer sheet to the upcoming State Quiz Bowl questions," Dr. Lopez replied, a hint of disappointment in her voice. "We received a tip late last night that your son stole it."

Dr. Lopez turned to face Jake.

"And you were such a wonderful ambassador for our public schools, Jake. I'm so disappointed."

"I don't know what you're talking about," Jake protested. "I didn't steal anything."

"Except this," said a police officer, coming out of Jake's bedroom, holding a blue booklet in his gloved hand. "The questions and answers to this week's State

Quiz Bowl competition. Says so right on the cover sheet."

"Where was it?" asked Dr. Lopez.

"Exactly where the tipster said it'd be. Hidden underneath the kid's Xbox console."

Dr. Lopez shook her head. "Is this how you won the district competition, Jake? By cheating?"

"No!" said Jake. "I wouldn't even know where to look for an answer sheet."

"At the offices of the State Quiz Bowl Alliance. They're the ones in charge of organizing the event."

"We found these in his desk, too," said the police officer. "Cheat guides for about six dozen different video games. Looks like cheating is a hobby for our young friend Jake here."

"Jake?" said his mom. All the pride had vanished from her watery eyes. "Did you do this thing?"

"Of course not. I mean, yeah, I used to look for shortcuts for my video games but—" He snapped his fingers. "Mrs. Malvolio!"

"Excuse me?" said the school superintendent. "What does your principal have to do with this?"

"She was here. Yesterday. She'd brought us a bunch of sequined T-shirts. And while she was here, somebody snuck into my room from the fire escape."

"Ha!" laughed the cop. "Kid, next time you make up an alibi, try to make it sound a little less ridiculous."

"Good advice," said Emma. She shook her head and walked away.

"Jake McQuade?" said Dr. Lopez, sounding like a hanging judge. "You are hereby barred from the River-view Middle School Quiz Bowl team. You are also suspended from school for a week."

55

Jake's mom grounded him, too.

He was "confined to quarters." That meant he could only come out of his bedroom for meals or to use the bathroom.

But that night, she let Grace and Kojo visit him in solitary confinement.

"Is this how you got so smart so fast?" demanded Grace, who seemed furious. "Do you have answer sheets for every single subject at school?"

"No," insisted Jake. "It was Mrs. Malvolio and her accomplices! You guys saw the closed window. You know she doesn't want us anywhere near the Quiz Bowl. Somebody broke in here while we were out in the living room dealing with her. They planted that evidence. That's how they could tell the police exactly where to find it."

Grace simmered down a little. She was willing to consider what Jake was saying.

"Well, how do we prove it?" she wondered.

"We could dust the windowsill for fingerprints!" said Kojo. "Maybe collect hair and fiber samples like they do on TV."

"Do you know how to do that, Kojo?" Jake asked eagerly.

"No."

Now Jake was frustrated. "You talk about all this detective and CSI stuff all the time but you can't do any of it?"

"Well," Kojo snapped back, "maybe if Haazim Farooqi made *me* a jar full of magical jelly beans, I could, baby. Maybe I could be a genius, just like you!"

Grace threw up her arms. "Who is Haazim Farooqi? And what's this about jelly beans?"

"That's how Jake got smart," blurted Kojo angrily. "Haazim Farooqi, who's this kooky mad scientist working in the subbasement of a building at Warwick College, was doing some kind of even kookier Ingestible Knowledge experiment, and Jake here accidentally became Subject One when he went to his mom's hotel and gobbled up a whole jar of jelly beans!"

Grace's mouth fell open.

"You just made that up, right?" she said.

Kojo shook his head. "Nope."

"It's true?" she asked.

Jake nodded. "Yeah. But I didn't know that the jelly beans were a knowledge delivery system."

"So you cheated. And these magical beans weren't enough? You had to steal the answer sheet, too?"

"For the last time," Jake pleaded, "I swear I didn't do it. I don't know how to steal anything."

"Oh yes, you do," said Grace. "After all, you're the smartest kid in the universe, remember?"

56

Late that night, Jake couldn't sleep.

He lay in his bed, staring at the ceiling. It was one of those bumpy ones, with what builders called a textured finish. As Jake studied the bumps, he started seeing patterns in the dots. Constellations of stars. Three-dimensional trigonometry problems. Vectors depicting advanced computer-aided design models for amazing new skyscrapers.

He wished he could turn his brain off.

He wished he'd never eaten those jelly beans.

He wished Grace, Kojo, his mom, and even Emma weren't so mad at him.

A little after eleven, his phone rang. It was Kojo.

"Hey," Jake said into his phone.

"Hey. I'm still not talking to you, but you need to turn on the news or crank up your computer."

"What's going on?"

"Big fire. Down at Warwick College. Corey Hall."

"That's where Haazim Farooqi has his lab!"

"I know."

"Is he okay?"

"I think so. They say there weren't any injuries, but I can't say for sure how Mr. Farooqi is doing, because he doesn't really call me. I'm not 'Subject One.'"

"Thanks for letting me know, Kojo."

"Yeah, whatever. Oh, by the way—Coach Lyons is disappointed in you, too. Says you're back to being the kid who forgets his uniform on game day because it's 'too much work' to remember stuff like that."

Kojo clicked off.

Jake went to his computer and searched for the latest news about the Corey Hall fire.

A fire in a subbasement chemistry lab was contained before it reached the upper floors of the college building, read the breaking-news bulletin. *The blaze was brought under control just before 10 p.m., but damage to the subbasement laboratory was extensive. No injuries were reported.*

Jake grabbed his phone and called Farooqi.

"Hello?"

"Haazim? It's me. Jake. Subject One. Are you okay?"

"Yes. Other than being temporarily lab-less and having my eyebrows singed, I'm fine. I might've used too many extension cords in my laboratory. There was some overheating and the smell of melting rubber. Then came the spark. The spark was not a good thing in a room full of chemicals and Bunsen burners. The entire room erupted into an indoor fireworks display."

"But you're okay?"

"I'm doing as well as can be expected, thank you for asking. However, my laboratory was completely destroyed. I was working on your jelly beans, Jake. But I can't tell you their formulas because the fire destroyed my computers. Melted them into smoldering lumps. The inferno also devoured my notes, my files, my chemicals, and my equipment. Everything. It's all gone. I'm lucky to be alive."

"I'm glad you weren't hurt."

"Thank you, Subject One. Unfortunately, I'm afraid this will delay our noble experiment. Everything I worked on for over a decade? Gone. Poof!"

"But you backed everything up, right?"

"Yes. That would've been a good idea. I wish I'd thought to do it before today. Oh, by the way, the college administrators have terminated my position as a research assistant."

"What? No way."

"Way. But don't worry, Jake. I have family. A sister in New Jersey. She and her husband have graciously agreed to let me live with them for a while. In their basement.

They don't want me doing experiments down there, of course, but that's okay. My PhD will just have to wait. I'll find a better-paying job and, after I make enough money, I'll rent a proper laboratory. One with smoke detectors and fire extinguishers. And then, when I make even more money, I'll buy a new computer and some chemicals and shiny new lab equipment. I'll make new and better jelly beans. If I did it once, I can do it again. It just might take another ten years."

"So," said Jake, "I hate to even bring this up, since I'm not the one who just lost his lab and job . . ."

"Temporary setbacks, my friend. I'll bounce back."

"But will I stay smart? Forever?"

"Yes, Subject One, I believe so. Unless, of course, the effects wear off, which I am starting to think won't happen due to the fact that you ingested so many IK capsules at once. I hypothesize that your brain will continue to experience fantastic knowledge leaps. Either that or it'll crash and burn."

"Mr. Farooqi?"

"Yes, Jake?"

"Why me?"

"Excuse me?"

"Why did I become Subject One?"

"Because, as you might recall, you ate my jelly beans."

"No, I mean—why weren't *you* the first test? Why didn't you try your IK capsules yourself?"

There was a long silence.

Finally, Farooqi sighed and answered Jake's question.

"Because I was afraid. You, on the other hand? You are very, very brave, Jake McQuade."

"No. I was just very, very hungry."

"I'm sorry. I have to go. My brother-in-law is here with his van. I'll talk to you again once my new laboratory is up and running. Goodbye, Subject One. And remember your promise: don't tell anyone of my involvement in this matter until I'm able to re-create the results."

Farooqi hung up.

Jake flopped back onto his bed.

He stared up at the bumpy ceiling and knew the new truth.

There was no returning to the Jake McQuade he used to be.

There was no antidote.

There never would be.

His life was a one-way street.

He could *look* back.

But he could never *go* back.

57

Since he was suspended from school for a week, Jake spent Monday morning alone in his room, studying the treasure map image on his phone, trying to learn Spanish from online videos.

If he was permanently cursed with superintelligence, he should probably use it to do something. Like help Emma with her homework.

"Hola, soy Lucía," said the nice lady on the computer screen. "Mucho gusto. Hi, I'm Lucía. Nice to meet you."

Lucía went on for a few hours. By the time she was done, Jake was surprised by how much he'd learned and retained—and not just how to find the bathroom or order an enchilada.

Emma, of course, had gone to school. Jake's mom was still home because she was working an event that night at the hotel. Tomorrow, Tuesday, she'd have to work a double shift.

"The State Quiz Bowl is still on for nine a.m. Wednesday," she'd told Jake when he had his breakfast of oatmeal (because it looked the most like the gruel they served in prisons and he sure felt like he was in prison). "You can't compete, of course. And they had to write all new questions with all new answers."

Around one o'clock in the afternoon, as Jake learned even more Spanish (the jelly beans had definitely increased his ability to learn more quickly), his mom knocked on his door.

"Jake? Kojo's here. He brought, uh, friends."

"Deputy Assistant Director Don Struchen, FBI," said a familiar voice.

"Special Agent Patrick Andrus," said another.

"Special Agent Sydney Tillman," said a third.

"Open this door," said Struchen. "We're here to investigate the crime scene."

Stunned, Jake opened the door. Kojo was standing on the other side with the three FBI agents. He was smiling with a white Tootsie Pop stick jutting out of the corner of his mouth. "Who loves ya, baby?"

"Uh, hi, Kojo. Hi, everybody. Qué bueno verles de nuevo. Great to see you again."

"Oh, you've been studying your Spanish?" said Kojo.

"Yeah," said Jake. "Doing it old-school."

"Good for you," said Kojo. "And you were right. When you said I should learn how to do some CSI stuff for real. I figured I could, if I had a teacher. Nobody really learns anything all by themselves."

"Your friend called us first thing this morning," explained the deputy assistant director, Mr. Struchen. "We owe you, Jake. Both of the Shaffer brothers are now behind bars for that bank robbery in California thanks to your brilliant work."

"Now, if you will please step out of the room," said Agent Tillman. She was toting a very large evidence-gathering kit. "We have work to do."

"Mr. Shelton?" said Agent Andrus. He had a laptop computer in a rugged military-style carrying case. "Would you care to observe?"

"Definitely!" said Kojo.

"What's your Wi-Fi password?" asked Andrus.

"Jellybeans," said Jake. "Lowercase. No space."

Jake and his mom waited in the living room while the three FBI agents and Kojo went to work. Two hours later, they emerged from the bedroom and started peeling off their sterile evidence-gathering gloves.

"Ms. McQuade?" said the deputy assistant director. "Your son was framed."

"Yes!" said Jake, doing a triumphant arm pump.

"We were able to lift some solid fingerprints off the windowsill and the Xbox console."

"We ran the fingerprints through our database," said

Special Agent Andrus, tapping his computer case. "We have a match."

Special Agent Tillman took up the narration. "One Eriq LeVisqueux. Seems like a strange crime for him to add to his rap sheet. LeVisqueux is a notorious international jewel thief and treasure hunter. The kind who would steal artifacts out of a sacred tomb and then sell them to the highest bidder."

"What was he doing here?" asked Jake's mom. "I don't have any valuable jewelry. . . ."

"We suspect that someone hired him, ma'am," said Agent Andrus.

"Jewel thieves, or second-story men as they are sometimes called, are good at climbing up fire escapes and crawling through partially open windows," added Agent Tillman.

"Someone hired LeVisqueux because they wanted your son out of the Quiz Bowl competition, Ms. McQuade," said Mr. Struchen. "Kojo here suspects one Patricia Malvolio. Apparently, she gave Monsieur LeVisqueux the distraction needed to draw the kids out of the bedroom."

"The school's principal?" said Jake's mom. "Why would she do a thing like that?"

"Because she wants the city to tear down our building and sell the land," said Jake. "She and her greedy uncle want the Riverview property for a luxury condominium complex."

"I need to make a few calls," said Mr. Struchen,

pulling out his phone. "We'll advise the local police to be on the lookout for LeVisqueux. He should be considered armed and dangerous. Tillman? Andrus?"

"Sir?" they said at the same time.

"I need you two to stay up here. Coordinate with the locals. LeVisqueux is wanted in fourteen states. His capture remains a federal matter."

"Yes, sir!"

"Ms. McQuade?" Struchen continued. "One final thing. Mr. Shelton here has requested that we call Dr. Lopez, the district superintendent, to advise her of our findings. With any luck, Jake will be going back to school tomorrow."

"And the day after that?" said Kojo, draping his arm over his friend's shoulder. "Me and Jake are back in the Quiz Bowl, baby!"

"Jake and *I*," Jake whispered.

"Whatever. Doesn't matter. We're back in the game!"

They were also back in the hunt.

The treasure hunt!

58

Because their mom had to work an event at the hotel, Jake and Emma ordered pizza for dinner.

Kojo and Grace came over to join them.

"Perdón por todas las cosas malas que dije," said Grace.

"No te apures," replied Jake. "Creo que yo hubiera dicho lo mismo."

"What?" said Grace. "You speak Spanish now."

"Little bit. And what you said wasn't all that mean."

"Did your friend Farooqi give you another smart jelly bean?"

"Who's Farooqi?" said Emma. "And what's this about jelly beans?"

"¡Nada!" said Jake. "I just spent the morning learning Spanish. On the computer."

"You spent the morning?" said Emma. "One morning?

227

I've been going to a Spanish-immersion school for *four* years!"

"El programa es muy bueno," said Jake, and everybody laughed. Except Kojo.

"What? What'd he say?"

"That it was a very good computer program," said Emma with a giggle.

"So good," said Jake, "I should be able to help you the next time you have a problem with your Spanish homework, Emma."

"¡Fantástico!"

"Anyway," said Grace, "I apologize, Jake. I said some mean things. And I put way too much pressure on you. There's nothing you could do to save the whole school by yourself. No great thing was ever accomplished without help."

"A very wise observation," said Jake. "Consider: Would we even know who Shakespeare was if a whole troupe of performers and stagecraft people hadn't helped him put on his plays?"

"Jake?" said Kojo. "Ease up, baby. You're getting all professorial on us again."

"Sorry."

After dinner, Jake, Kojo, and Grace reconvened in Jake's bedroom.

"I don't care how hot it gets," said Kojo. "Tonight we are leaving that window closed and locked."

"That was smart of you to call the FBI, Kojo," said Grace.

Kojo nodded and took in a chest-ballooning breath. "Yep. It's like you said. No great thing is ever done solo. Sometimes we have to bump these things up to the next level. The feds have more resources than I do."

"I've been thinking," said Jake. "It's not a coincidence that the guy who broke in here, Monsieur Eriq LeVisqueux, is a notorious jewel thief *and* treasure hunter. I'm guessing he'll be the guy Huxley hires to go down into the caves to find the pirate treasure."

"But," said Grace, "he doesn't have the cabin boy's clue!"

"Or," said Kojo, "that treasure map we drew up."

"It's not a great map," said Jake, sounding frustrated. "I've been staring at it all day, in between Spanish lessons. How do we find 'X' if the location of the fire pit remains unknown? The whole puzzle starts with the fire pit. . . ."

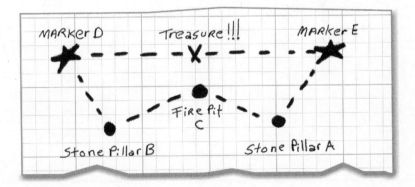

"You guys want dessert?" Emma came into the room with a stack of bowls, a half gallon of chocolate chip cookie dough ice cream, and a scooper. "Huh. What're you working on?"

"No es nada," said Jake, covering up the word *treasure* on his graph paper with a rubber eraser.

"It looks like a geometry problem," said Emma. "Aren't you guys supposed to learn geometry in middle school?"

"Of course!" said Jake. "Emma? ¡Eres la mejor hermana del mundo!"

Emma smiled. "Gracias. You're a pretty good big brother, too."

"What's going on?" said Kojo as Emma scooped out the ice cream. "Are you having a brainstorm or do you just really, really like chocolate chip cookie dough ice cream?"

"Brainstorm," said Jake. "You guys are right. We can't do this alone. We need help. We need Mr. Keeney!"

59

Early Tuesday morning, before the first bell rang, Jake headed to homeroom.

Mr. Keeney was already at his desk, reading another paperback science fiction book.

"Mr. Keeney?" said Jake after rapping his knuckles on the doorjamb. "Hate to bother you . . ."

"That's okay, Jake," he said, closing his book. "The forces around the Outer Rim territories have come together to fight the Yuuzhan Vong. Luke Skywalker should show up soon. Great to have you back with us."

"Thanks."

"So jewel thieves broke into your apartment?"

"That's what the FBI says."

"That is so awesome. How can I help you?"

"I have this geometry problem."

"You do? When I was your age, all I had was a girl problem."

"Yeah. I might have one of those, too. Here's the math problem."

Jake spread out his graph paper on the teacher's desk. He'd redone it without the word *treasure* written over the X or any of the other notations.

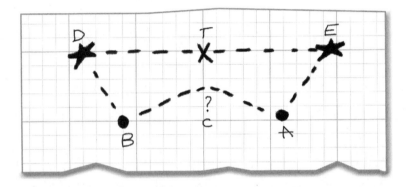

"Oooh," said Mr. Keeney, rubbing his hands together. "Fascinating. What do we know about the relationship between all these points?"

Jake recited the clues, editing out words like *stone pillars, fire pit,* and *pirate's treasure*—keeping it all very geometry-ish, with points and angles and lines.

"What do you know about imaginary numbers, plane geometry, and vector algebra, Jake?"

"Not enough, sir."

Mr. Keeney blasted off like one of the rocket ships in his *Star Wars* novels. "You don't need to know where 'C,' 'D,' or 'E' is to find 'T.'"

By the time the first bell rang, Mr. Keeney had moved on to "Since we know the sides of our triangle are equal lengths, we can factor the isosceles equality of the vectors." As kids came into homeroom, they joined Jake behind Mr. Keeney's desk so they could watch the math whiz at work.

Just like he had with his internet Spanish lessons, Jake caught on pretty quickly to what Mr. Keeney was saying. After a few minutes, he was able to understand strange new concepts. The jelly bean–lubricated synapses in his brain were soaking it all in. Jake started adding in vectors and angles and working the equations along with Mr. Keeney.

"Multiplying by i turns the vector ninety degrees to the left and does not change the length," Jake said.

"Precisely!" said Mr. Keeney, rolling up his sleeves. "You remind me of a young me, Jake!"

"Thank you, sir."

"Hmm, I don't know if you should thank me. Being a math nerd led to those girl problems I told you about."

"Things are different now, sir. Nerds rock."

Ten minutes and lots of complicated formulae and triangles and vectors and a few multiplications by pi later, they had found X (which Jake had also labeled T for *treasure*)—without having to worry about where the fire pit (C) was.

When the problem was solved, Mr. Keeney stood up behind his desk, clutching his pencil in his hand as if it were a microphone.

CANCELS OUT

$(Z_D - Z_B)i = Z_E - Z_B$

$(Z_A - Z_D)i = Z_D - Z_A$

$(Z_A - Z_B)i = Z_E + Z_D - (Z_B + Z_A)$

VECTOR SUM

T MIDPOINT

$\dfrac{Z_E + Z_D}{2}$

? c

E   B   A   D

MIDPOINT T   MIDPOINT OF B & A

$\dfrac{Z_E + Z_D}{2} = \dfrac{Z_B + Z_A}{2} + i\,\dfrac{Z_A + Z_B}{2}$

90° ROTATION OF MIDPOINT

BA

DON'T NEED TO KNOW LOCATION OF C

T

B   A

½ DISTANCE BETWEEN B AND A THEN A 90° ROTATION AT B (REPRESENTED BY i IN THE EQUATION)

T IS LOCATED AT THE 4TH VERTEX OF THE SQUARE CREATED BY THE MIDPOINT OF THE LINE BETWEEN B AND A!

"If you use imaginary numbers, you don't need to know where 'C' is to find 'T.' All you need are 'A' and 'B.' And that, my friends," he said to the room full of fascinated students, "is how we bring the geometry! Boo-yah!"

He opened his hand and the pencil dropped to the floor.

Everybody cheered.

Jake was cheering the loudest.

Because his map was complete. If Mr. Keeney could find *T* without knowing where *C* was, so could Jake.

He could find the treasure without the fire pit!

He'd just have to bring his mad new math skills with him into the cave.

60

Mrs. Malvolio stepped out of her office when she saw Jake McQuade, Kojo Shelton, and Grace Garcia walking toward the exit.

She blocked their path.

"No after-school activities for you three today?" she asked with one of her lipstick-crinkling smiles.

"No," said Kojo, answering for the group. "We're just gonna head home and chillax. Big morning tomorrow. The Quiz Bowl starts at nine o'clock sharp."

"We probably won't be wearing those shirts you dropped off at my apartment the other night," said Jake. "You know, the night the thief broke into my bedroom during the exact same time you were with us in the living room."

"I heard about that!" said Mrs. Malvolio. "What an odd coincidence."

"You can say that again," said Kojo.

Mrs. Malvolio almost did. But then she caught herself.

"Almost as odd as Grace getting sick right after she ate your brownies," added Jake.

"Yes, I've been wondering about that, too," said Mrs. Malvolio, placing a hand over her heart. "It's almost as if someone tainted my brownies when I wasn't looking."

"Yeah," said Kojo sarcastically. "It's *almost* like that."

"We think the shirts are a little too splashy," said Grace. "Too showy. We don't want to look conceited when we win."

"No, I suppose not. Tell me, Jake, have the authorities apprehended this Monsieur Eriq LeVisqueux fellow?"

"Not yet."

"Good, good," Mrs. Malvolio muttered to herself.

"Excuse me?" said Grace.

"I was just remarking that it's good that you three look so good. Are you sure you still want to do the Quiz Bowl? I mean, after all you've been through. All your families have been through. Especially yours, Jake. Your poor mother."

"She's good," said Jake. "We're good."

"My family's super cool," said Kojo. "They like how I can add 'worked with the FBI' on all my college applications."

"My family is fine, too, Mrs. Malvolio," said Grace. "In fact, my uncle Charley has never been better. He's about to become something of a hero. Let's just say that tomorrow mi tío hará que sus antepasados se sientan muy, muy orgullosos."

"Right," said Mrs. Malvolio, blinking some more. "Let's just say that, shall we?"

She watched the three friends boldly stride out the exit. She could tell by their jiggling shoulders that they were snickering at her. Probably because they thought que no podía hablar español.

But she did. She hablaba español like nobody's business.

So she knew the annoying little brats were going to go digging for Dog Breath's booty that very night.

Because brainy little Grace had said that tomorrow "mi tío hará que sus antepasados se sientan muy, muy orgullosos."

Meaning that tomorrow her uncle, Charley Lyons, the direct descendant of the Cubano cabin boy Eduardo Leones, was going to "make his ancestors very, very proud."

The children were going down into the cave to retrieve *her* family's treasure. She needed to alert her uncle Heath and his hired help, Eriq LeVisqueux.

She needed to alert them immediately.

The race was on!

61

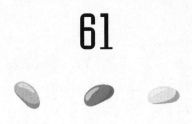

Grace, Jake, and Kojo worked out an elaborate scheme for not being at their own homes on Tuesday night.

They each told their parents that they'd be spending the night with their teammates "so we can keep cramming for the Quiz Bowl up to the last second."

Jake told his mom that he'd be at Kojo's. Kojo told his folks he'd be at Jake's. Grace told her mom and dad that everybody was bunking at Uncle Charley's place because, since he was the vice principal, he had the keys they'd need if they had to go borrow books from the school library.

At precisely eleven p.m., they all reconvened in the unlit parking lot behind the school. Mr. Lyons had told them to wait for him at the cafeteria loading dock because he knew the security camera back there was broken. They wouldn't have to worry about Mrs. Malvolio or Mr. Huxley seeing what they were up to.

The heavy metal service door slowly swung open.

"Grace?"

"Yeah, Uncle Charley. Jake and Kojo, too."

"Good to see you guys," he whispered. "Follow me. We have to take a circuitous route to my office. That way we can avoid all the cameras."

Mr. Lyons led Jake, Grace, and Kojo on a serpentine path through the cafeteria and the corridors. In one hall, they had to zig and zag to opposite sides and sidle along the lockers to avoid the security cameras. Finally they made it into the old custodian's closet, Mr. Lyons's office.

"Help me push this aside," he said, placing his hands on one edge of a stacked filing cabinet. Everybody found a spot to help shove.

"On three. One, two, three . . ."

They dug in their heels and drove the heavy thing sideways. When they did, they exposed a rusty metal door. There was an ancient school-bus-yellow sign with a black circle holding three equilateral yellow triangles. Below the circle were boldface yellow letters on a black background spelling FALLOUT SHELTER.

"This is the entrance," said Mr. Lyons. "The path down to the double rock pillar chamber is simple. When you reach the four forks in the paths and crawl spaces and have to make a choice, remember: right, right, left, left."

"Right, right, left, left," said Jake.

"Right."

"There's a third right?" said Kojo.

"No," said Grace. "Two rights, then two lefts."

Mr. Lyons nodded. "Right."

"So there *is* another right after the last left?" said Kojo.

"No," said Grace. "It's just right, right, left, left."

"Correct," said Jake before Mr. Lyons could say "right" again.

"Okay," said Kojo. "Got it. Now explain that bit about 'crawl spaces.'"

"The final approach to the treasure chamber," said Mr. Lyons, "is a very tight squeeze. You will need to crawl."

"Like on our bellies?"

"Exactly."

"Quick question," said Jake. "If the passageways are that confined and narrow, how did the cabin boy ever drag the pirate's treasure down to the chamber in the first place?"

"Very slowly. Maybe one sack of gold or jewelry at a time."

"Guess that's how we'll have to carry it out, too," said Grace.

"Good thing the Quiz Bowl doesn't start till nine o'clock in the morning," cracked Kojo. "We've got, what? Ten whole hours to find the treasure, dig it up, and haul everything out."

"Nine hours and forty-five minutes," said Jake, glancing at his watch. "We've already burned through fifteen."

"Then let's go," said Grace.

"Here," said Mr. Lyons. "I brought these in from home. Two shovels and a pickax."

Jake and Kojo arched their eyebrows.

"I like to garden on the weekends. You'll need tools to dig up the treasure. This, too." He handed Grace a tape measure, which she clipped to her jeans.

"You're not coming with us?" she asked.

"Can't. Bad back. I'd never make it through the crawl space. Here. You'll need these, too." He handed them flashlights. "I'll stay up here and guard the entrance. After all, even though I'm the vice principal, I'm also the custodian."

"A person who has responsibility for or looks after something," said Jake.

"That's right," said Mr. Lyons. "And when you kids find the treasure, I will become the Last Custodian."

"The Last Custodian," said Kojo, framing the words dramatically in the air. "That sounds like a good title for a *Star Wars* movie. Come on, you guys. We've got some right-right, left-left turning and belly crawling to do!"

62

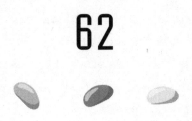

At first the going was pretty easy.

The cinder-block corridor was maybe four feet wide and eight feet tall. Lightbulbs inside wire cages lined the walls every ten feet. Ductwork and pipes were fastened to the ceiling.

"This must be the route to the old fallout shelter from the nineteen sixties," said Grace.

"Makes sense," said Jake, who was carrying the pickax. Kojo and Grace each had a shovel.

"You think there's any, like, canned food in the shelter?" asked Kojo, his voice ringing off the walls. "Maybe some Spam or SpaghettiOs? Because I was so excited about sneaking out of the house tonight to go treasure hunting, I didn't eat any dinner."

"We don't have time for a snack break," said Grace as they entered a long, dimly lit cinder-block room. There were rusty cots holding the mouse-chewed remains of mattresses lined up against one long wall. Metal barrels the size of oil drums labeled SURVIVAL SUPPLIES DRINKING WATER were stacked in a corner. There were also moldy cardboard crates filled with cans of something called BISCUIT, SURVIVAL, ALL-PURPOSE.

"Saltines," mumbled Kojo, blowing away a thick coating of dust to inspect an open canister. "You'd need to drink a barrel of that water over there after you ate one of these dry crackers."

"We have a choice up ahead," said Grace, pointing to the far end of the shelter. "Two doors."

"Two exits," said Jake.

"We take the one on the right," said Kojo. "Right?"

"Yes!" said Jake and Grace.

"Okay, that's our first right, right?"

"Correct!" Jake and Grace said that together, too.

The team made it to the doorway on the right, which, of course, was closed. It took all three of them, and several grunts, to shove open the heavy metal panel. It screeched on its hinges the whole way.

On the other side, a new kind of passageway presented itself. This one seemed to be a natural crevice slicing through slick, smooth stone.

"No lights," said Jake, flicking on his flashlight. "This is an actual cave."

"I wish Uncle Charley had brought me down here years ago!" said Grace. "This cavern is awesome!"

The beam shuddered when Jake jumped because he heard a shrieking sound behind him.

Kojo was trying to push the thick door shut. He made it halfway.

"Leave it open," said Grace. "We'll be coming out this same way."

"Okay," said Kojo. "But my mother always gives me grief when I leave a door open. Especially if the air conditioner is running."

They hiked down the much narrower passageway.

Water plinked. What sounded like bat wings fluttered. Jake swung up his flashlight and illuminated several tapering stone icicles suspended from the ceiling of the cave.

"Those are stalactites, formed of calcium salts deposited by dripping water. The ones jutting up from the floor are called stalagmites. One way to tell them apart is this simple mnemonic device—"

"Jake?" said Kojo before his friend could launch into explaining his memorization trick. "You're doing it again."

"Well, this mnemonic device is extremely clever."

"Go on," said Grace, rolling her eyes.

"A stalactite holds *tight* to the ceiling," said Jake proudly. "A stalagmite *might* climb up to the ceiling someday."

Grace and Kojo remained silent.

Finally, Kojo exploded. "That's it?"

"Uh, yeah."

"You think that's clever? We're in a cave, on a treacherous treasure hunt, and you—"

Kojo didn't get to complete that thought.

Because, behind them, someone had just pushed open that screechy steel door.

Someone was following them.

63

Jake doused his flashlight, tucked it into his belt, and grabbed Grace's right hand with his left.

She grabbed Kojo's.

Jake used his right hand to feel along the cold stone wall and lead his friends to the fork in the path. He instantly knew that's how to find the way through any simply connected maze: follow the right wall. It would also lead them to the next "right" they were supposed to make.

Behind them, he heard something clacking.

One of Mrs. Malvolio's chunky necklaces!

"Are you absolutely sure this is the right way, Monsieur LeVisqueux?"

"Oui, Madame Malvolio. I have zee sixth sense for zees things. Eet is why you will be giving me ten percent of zee treasure when I find eet for vous."

"Then hurry up," growled Heath Huxley. "Those thieving little brats have a head start!"

Jake, Kojo, and Grace followed the cave path to the right. They slid up against the stone wall and froze.

"Up there, you see where zee passageway splits? We will, of course, take zee tunnel on . . . zee left."

Jake breathed a silent sigh of relief and finally let go of Grace's hand. He waited for the chattering voices of LeVisqueux, Huxley, and Malvolio to fade away. They were deep down the tunnel worming through the caverns in the opposite direction.

"They're going the wrong way," whispered Kojo.

"Let's hope they knew about another entrance to the fallout shelter. Otherwise . . ."

"They could've hurt Uncle Charley!" said Grace.

"Exactly," said Jake. "We should head back. Make sure he's okay."

"No," said Grace. "He'd want us to claim the treasure first. It's been his goal his whole life. But we need to move fast. We'll find the treasure, record our discovery on video, and bring up one or two pieces to prove our claim. We can come back for the rest after we make sure Uncle Charley is okay and the treasure is officially declared ours."

"How does that happen?" said Kojo.

"By invoking the 'treasure trove' notion of common law," said Jake. "It refers to any property that is verifiably antiquated and has been concealed for so long that the owner is probably dead or unknown and certainly unlikely to demand that their goods be returned. In such an instance, 'finders keepers' would apply."

"Okay," said Kojo. "That kind of brainy brain fart I like. Keep that kind comin'. Let's go."

The team made their way up the slick fissure.

"Another split, you guys," said Grace.

"This time we go left," said Kojo. "Right?"

"Correct!" said Grace and Jake. "Left."

The arched passageway took them into another chamber.

There was smelly slime on the floor.

"Bat guano," said Jake.

"What's guano?" asked Kojo.

"A fancy word for 'poop,' " said Grace.

"Gross, man," said Kojo, trying to high-step his way across the floor to avoid the sticky puddles of brown bat doo.

"As a manure," Jake started, "bat guano is an extremely effective fertilizer, thanks to its exceptionally high levels of nitrogen, phosphate, and—"

"Jake?" This time it was Grace who cut him off. "Nobody wants to know that right now."

"Sorry. My bad."

"Where are all the bats?" asked Kojo, swinging his flashlight beam up to the ceiling.

"It's night," said Jake. "Bats go to work at night. They 'see' in the dark using a special skill called echolocation. It's a little like sonar in that—"

"Jake?!" Kojo and Grace said it together.

"Sorry. Something about the adrenaline associated with this treasure hunt has shifted my brain into hyperdrive."

"Try to save it until we need it," urged Grace. "There. Another split. Two holes. See them?"

"Where?" said Kojo, swinging his flashlight back and forth.

"Aim lower," said Grace, spotlighting the pair of tunnels with her dusty beam.

"Welcome to the crawl space," said Kojo, shaking his head.

"We take the one on the left," said Jake.

"And," added Kojo, "we crawl on our bellies."

64

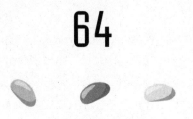

The crawl space was tight, with a slanted ceiling covered with tiny saw-toothed stalactites.

Jake had to drag the heavy pickax behind him. Crawling with the thing was like trying to swim while tugging an anchor.

"It opens up," reported Grace, who had taken the lead for the belly-sliding portion of the trek. She heaved her shovel forward with a clang. "I can see the room. It's the treasure chamber! I can see one of the rock pillars."

Jake and Kojo scooted faster, working their legs and arms to crawl forward as quickly as they could.

"I'm in!" called Grace, her voice echoing off the high ceiling of the treasure chamber. Kojo popped out second. Jake brought up the rear.

"Whoa." The three of them stood in awe, swinging their flashlights across the stalactite-dripping ceiling, admiring the vast cathedral of glittering stone they'd just entered.

The whole floor was covered with a sea of rubble.

"What's up with the floor?" said Kojo.

"To bury treasure in a cave with a stone floor," suggested Grace, "you'd have to chisel out a vault of stone. To hide that vault, you'd need to cover the floor with a carpet of pebbles."

Jake knelt down and worked his hand through the small stones. "I'm up to my elbow and I haven't even hit solid stone yet."

"Eduardo Leones worked long and hard to hide his treasure," said Grace with great admiration.

"There are the two rock pillars!" said Kojo. "Just like in the riddle!"

"And, of course, there's no fire pit," said Grace.

"Okay," Kojo said to Jake, "now's the time to fire up your brain, baby. We need a little extra-credit math work out of you ASAP."

Jake examined the tower of stacked rocks on the right.

"Huh," he said. "Some of these rocks have words chiseled into them. Spanish words."

Kojo came over with his phone up. "I'm shooting video."

"Don't waste too much of your battery," said Grace. "We really need to document the moment when we raise the treasure from its ancient hiding place to establish our claim."

"Gotcha." Kojo tapped the red dot to stop recording. Meanwhile, Jake had started pulling the word stones out of the pile. He placed them on the cave floor.

"Um, shouldn't you be doing some geometry or something?" said Kojo.

"In a minute. These word stones aren't here by coincidence. They could be another clue."

Jake lined the words up in a random order.

OTRO PUEDES SIEMPRE CAMINO ENCONTRAR

He started translating: " 'Other you can always way find.' "

"That makes absolutely no sense, Jake," said Grace. "I know you just learned Spanish yesterday, but come on." She hunkered down and quickly rearranged the stones to construct a different sentence.

SIEMPRE PUEDES ENCONTRAR OTRO CAMINO

" 'You can always find another way,' " said Jake, reading what Grace had written with the rocks. "Of course!"

"Of course what?" said Kojo.

"There never was a fire pit! Your ancestor was a genius, Grace. A math prodigy. The cabin boy knew how to do plane geometry and trigonometry, maybe even better than Mr. Keeney. All along, there was only one way to find his buried treasure! With math!"

65

Grace and Kojo measured the distance between the two rock pillars.

Jake found a rocky ledge, sat down, and jotted their findings in the small notebook he'd stuffed into his back pocket before leaving home. He'd remembered to bring a pencil, of course, and a plastic pig-shaped pencil sharpener. (He'd borrowed it from Emma.)

"There are more word stones in this second rock pillar," reported Grace.

"What do they say?" Jake called across the cavernous chamber.

"The same thing. 'You can always find another way.'"

"So that's the only measurement we can take," said Kojo. "From rock pillar A to rock pillar B. The rest is up to you, Jake."

"And Eduardo Leones," added Jake. He had written

the full text of the cabin boy's clue on the inside of the notebook's front cover.

Jake went to work.

It took ten minutes for him to re-create the solution he'd figured out with Mr. Keeney, this time factoring in the actual spacing between the two rock pillars which had been missing until now.

By one a.m., he was ready to transfer the data from his pencil sketch map to the actual cave floor. He started pacing through the sea of chunky gravel.

"Let me know when to start recording video again," said Kojo.

Jake didn't answer. He was laser-focused on the map, which he could see without even looking down at his notebook. It was as if his eyes had a fighter pilot's head-up guidance system projected in front of them. He could see the grid, the intersecting lines and triangles, glowing green on the floor.

He could see the X from the geometry puzzle.

He stopped on the spot.

"Grab your shovels, guys. This is where we dig."

Jake swung the pickax to break up the gravel, which had cemented itself together with caked dust.

"Roll camera!" shouted Grace.

Kojo set his phone on a rocky outcropping on the nearest cave wall and started recording.

"Welcome to our glorious treasure recovery, folks!" he said to the camera. "Stay tuned for pirate booty, baby."

Grace and Kojo grabbed shovels and moved load after load of crushed stone up and out of the way. They sank their blades into the sea of stone—loosened by swings of Jake's pick—and heaved it backward in a pitter-pattering shower of gravel. It took time, but soon, working together, they dug a four-feet-wide, two-feet-deep hole in the floor.

"How much deeper?" asked Kojo, swiping sweat off his brow.

"Eduardo didn't tell us," said Jake, busting up another chunk of stone with the sharp metal tip of his tool.

He heard a *tink*.

Metal hitting metal.

He looked at Grace, who looked at Kojo, who looked back at Jake.

In a flash, the three friends fell to their knees. They scooped up pebbles with their bare hands and tossed them up over the edge of the hole.

"It's a metal trunk!" shouted Kojo when its dusty top revealed itself. "A treasure chest!"

They scraped away more stones until the entire top was uncovered.

There was a rusty hasp—a slotted hinged metal plate—fitted over a loop for a lock, but there was no lock.

"Pry it up," said Jake. "We can use the hasp as a lever to open this lid."

Grace used the pointed edge of her shovel to pop up the hasp.

The three friends scrambled out of the shallow pit so they weren't standing on top of the treasure chest's lid.

"You do it, Grace," said Jake. "After all, the cabin boy is *your* ancestor. This treasure belongs to you and your family."

"Minus ten percent," added Kojo.

Grace reached down. Grabbed hold of the hasp. "This is for you, Great-to-the-eighth-power Uncle Eduardo. You too, Uncle Charley. Hang on. We're coming!"

She pulled with all her might.

The lid squealed open.

"Wow!" the three friends gasped.

The giant metal box was overflowing with glittery, twinkling treasure. Stacks of shimmering gold coins. Mountains of sparkling jewels. A silver candelabra, an emerald necklace, and even a diamond-encrusted crown.

And that was just the top layer of treasure in the very deep chest.

"We did it, baby!" Kojo shouted to where he knew his phone camera was watching. "We just dug up Dog Breath's booty!"

Grace joined him, tossing two handfuls of gold coins up into the air. "We sure did!"

Jake added a "Woo-hoo!" to the camera, showing it the emerald necklace he'd plucked out of the treasure chest.

The three laughed so hard they had tears in their eyes.

They sank to the floor, scooping up loot and plopping it by the handfuls into their laps.

"Uncle Charley can retire," said Grace. "He can buy his own private island!"

"I'm going to buy a new chemistry set," said Kojo.

"I'm going to pay for Mr. Farooqi to get his PhD!"

"This treasure has to be worth millions!" exclaimed Grace. "We can definitely help fix up the school."

"Heck," said Kojo. "You can fix up two schools. Maybe three. You could build a brand-new school on top of the old school."

Behind them, Jake heard beads clacking.

"No, children," said a very familiar voice. "That is not going to happen."

Mrs. Malvolio had just crawled into the chamber.

Mr. Huxley and the notorious treasure hunter Eriq LeVisqueux came crawling out right behind her.

LeVisqueux was brandishing a sword.

He was, as the FBI had predicted, armed and dangerous.

66

"Zees is my favorite way to hunt for zee treasure," laughed LeVisqueux, swishing his saber in the air. "Let some other fool find eet, and zen steal eet out from under zem."

"Thanks for doing our digging, kids," chuckled Mr. Huxley.

"I'll make sure you all get extra credit for it," joked Mrs. Malvolio.

"We found the treasure," said Grace. "Therefore, it's ours."

"Not if we steal it from you first," said Mr. Huxley. "You see, little girl, this treasure belonged to my great-great-great-great-great-great-great-great-grandfather Alonso Mieras."

"Whoa," said Kojo. "That's a lot of *great*s. I mean, can any grandfather be *that* good?"

"Silence, foolish boy!" Eriq LeVisqueux slashed his blade through the air again.

"My bad. Please continue, sir."

Huxley took a dramatic step forward. "My grandfather's name was Miguel Mieras. His ancestor, Alonso, was the pirate known and feared across the seven seas as Capitán Aliento de Perro! Captain Dog Breath!"

When he made that proclamation, Mrs. Malvolio fanned the air beneath her nose. "Did somebody step in that bat guano in the other room?"

Mr. Huxley ignored her. "This treasure you claim to be yours? It belongs to my family."

"No, it doesn't!" said Grace. "Your ancestor, Dog Breath, stole it in a mutiny from the real captain of the ship—*my* ancestor, the brave buccaneer Angel Vengador Leones!"

"So?" said Mr. Huxley. "They were pirates. They stole stuff. My ancestor stole it last!"

"No, the real captain's son, Eduardo, did."

"Aha! You admit he was a thief!"

"He was a pirate!"

"None of that matters," said Jake. "We found it first. And, if I might cite the common law principle governing this sort of treasure salvage, it clearly states—"

"Sacré bleu!" shouted LeVisqueux. "Enough! We must move swiftly."

"True," said Mrs. Malvolio, checking her watch. "It's nearly two o'clock in the morning. I have to be at the

Imperial Marquis for that silly Quiz Bowl competition in less than seven hours. I think I'll resign as principal right after my poor, tumbledown school embarrasses itself at the state finals. Oh yes. We're going to lose. Because our champion Quiz Bowl team—poof—disappeared."

LeVisqueux dumped the contents of his knapsack on the floor: a rope, some pinions, a pair of pulleys, and a stack of nylon tote bags with drawstring tops.

"Did you children bring bags and rope to haul out zee treasure?" he asked. "No. Of course not. You are zee amateurs. I am zee professional. Zees is zee only way to haul all zee gold and jewels out of zees chamber. Quickly now, load up zees bags with everything you have found." He wiggled his sword. "Do eet now—or else!"

Grace, Kojo, and Jake reluctantly loaded up the bags. It took over an hour to pack everything into the bulging sacks. The whole time, Jake was hoping his big brain would come up with a way out of this jam. So far, it hadn't.

LeVisqueux attached a pulley to a pinion he'd staked into the cave floor, then looped a cord through the pulley's wheels. He worked up a sweat and wiped his brow with a knit cap he pulled out of his pants pocket.

"I will take zee line to zee other side of zee crawl space. You two—tie zee treasure bags to zee rope and I will pull zem into zee far chamber with me."

"I'm going with you," said Mr. Huxley, sounding as if he didn't trust LeVisqueux. "Patricia? Grab the sword and keep an eye on the kids."

"What'd you creeps do to Uncle Charley?" Grace blurted.

"Oh, he's fine," said Mrs. Malvolio. "I'm sure he'd be coming down to rescue you if he weren't sound asleep and all tied up at the moment. Probably will be until somebody goes looking for him. Of course, nobody is coming to school today. I sent out an email blast. School is cancelled so everybody can go support you three at the Quiz Bowl. Too bad you won't be there to hear them cheer you on."

67

Jake couldn't believe they were being forced to help the bad guys steal the treasure.

But they didn't have a choice.

Half an hour later, fifty nylon bags filled with gold coins, jewelry, rare gems, and precious artifacts had been shuttled out of the chamber through the crawl space.

"Thank you all for your assistance," giggled Mrs. Malvolio. "Hopefully, you will be happy in your new middle schools since, after Riverview's miserable showing at the Quiz Bowl and the tragic outcome of your unchaperoned adventure down here in these dangerous caves, aided by, of all people, the vice principal, the school board will have no choice but to shutter Riverview and bulldoze it to the ground!"

She chuckled maniacally.

"Oh, who am I kidding? You three are never going

back to school. But your deaths shall not be in vain. We will use all this treasure to finance the most spectacular high-rise condo this city has ever seen. It will be our castle in the sky!" She crouched down, keeping the tip of the sword pointed at Grace, then Kojo, then Jake, then back to Grace. "Uncle Heath?" she hollered into the crawl space. "Haul me out of here. Fast!"

"Grab hold of the line!" Huxley shouted back. "Pull, Eriq, pull!"

"Oui, monsieur, oui!"

Mrs. Malvolio flopped onto her back. She dropped the sword so she could grab hold of the moving rope with both hands. She slid out of the chamber like one of the lumpy treasure sacks, bouncing along over the bumpy cave floor.

"Ooh," she cried. "Ouch. That hurt. Oooh again."

"This is our chance!" said Kojo, racing across the floor to grab the weapon.

"Leave it!" Grace and Jake both shouted.

Kojo skidded to a stop.

"Get away from the mouth of that passageway!" said Jake.

"Why?"

"Because, you idiot," shouted Mrs. Malvolio, safe on the other side. "We also brought dynamite!"

"Dynamite?!"

Kojo dashed back across the chamber as fast as he could and dove behind the first pillar of stones. Grace and Jake ducked behind the other one.

A tremendous *KABOOM!* roared out of the crawl space, followed by a cannon blast of dust and debris. The narrow passageway's ceiling splintered and crumbled. There was an avalanche of boulders inside the slanted tunnel.

The exit was completely blocked. Sealed.

There was no way out.

"Okay," said Kojo when the dust finally settled. "I'm wishing I would've dragged some of those survival crackers down here with me."

"Did your phone survive the explosion?" asked Jake.

"Why are you interested in his phone when we're about to die?" wondered Grace.

"Because that phone is video evidence that we found the treasure first. That Mrs. Malvolio and her uncle stole it from us."

"With a little help from their Frenchy friend," added Kojo, who'd gone to the rock ledge to examine his phone. "It's all good," he reported. "We got the whole thing on video. I wish I could email it to my friends at the FBI, but the Wi-Fi down here is terrible. Cell service, too. There is none."

"I hope Uncle Charley is okay," said Grace.

"Mrs. Malvolio said he is," said Jake. "They wouldn't kill him."

"But he can identify them," said Grace.

"Doubtful," said Jake. "Remember, LeVisqueux is a pro. My guess? He probably wore the ski mask he used to to wipe sweat off his brow and he blindfolded your uncle before Huxley and Malvolio even entered his office. It'll just look like a botched burglary. They don't want a murder on their hands."

"Except ours," said Kojo.

"Uncle Charley will tell the police that we're down here," said Grace eagerly. "When he wakes up, he'll call nine-one-one. We're going to be rescued!"

"Maybe," said Jake.

"Um, what do you mean by 'maybe'?" wondered Kojo.

"Mrs. Malvolio seemed super confident that *we* weren't going to crawl out of this cave and testify against them. Therefore, logic forces me to conclude that they brought down more dynamite to seal up more of the cave."

Just then, as if on cue, the cavernous chamber's walls shuddered. A few stalactite spears lost their grip on the ceiling and plummeted, shattering on the rock-strewn floor like falling icicles in a thaw. One or two barely missed Jake and Grace. Kojo's hair was full of dust.

"Do you have to know everything?" said Kojo. "I think I liked you better when you were just, you know, *you*."

Jake nodded.

Even though he didn't agree with what Kojo just said.

If he wasn't the smartest kid in the universe, he might not be able to figure out an alternate escape route.

Which he hadn't done yet.

But he was definitely working on it.

68

Hours passed.

To conserve their batteries, Jake suggested that everybody turn off their flashlights.

The chilled stone chamber, which felt like some kind of tomb, was plunged into total darkness. Jake could hear Kojo sobbing. Grace sniffled some, too.

None of them said much. They were lost in their thoughts.

A new one percolated up in Jake's brain.

You can always find another way.

The message written in stone from the rock pillars. Both of them.

Why had Eduardo Leones repeated himself like that?

The first "another way" was the math problem. If there never was a fire pit, the cabin boy knew that to find his treasure, his descendants would need to explore another way of solving the problem. They'd have to use the plane geometry solution. They could imagine a virtual fire pit at any random point. Its true location was irrelevant to finding the treasure.

But what was the second "another way"?

Wait a minute.

Jake's buzzing brain made another connection, another leap.

If the bad guys had to ferry the loot out of the treasure room in fifty nylon tote bags attached to a rope-and-pulley system, how the heck did young Eduardo Leones haul a heavy metal treasure chest the size of an old-fashioned steamer trunk into the room?

The thing was a four-by-four-by-four cube. No way could it fit through the crawl space.

You can always find another way.

Another way into the chamber.

Which, of course, meant there was also another way *out* of the chamber.

The fire pit!

The missing point in the puzzle. Maybe it never was a fire pit. Maybe that was just Leones's clever code for an escape hatch.

Jake flicked on his flashlight.

"I thought we weren't supposed to be burning batteries," said Grace, snapping hers on, too.

"I need to do some more math," Jake explained. "I

think there *is* a fire pit, only it's not really a pozo de fuego. More like una escotilla de escape. An escape hatch!"

Kojo's flashlight clicked on. "What's this about an escape hatch?"

"I think there's a second entrance and exit in this room," said Jake. "How else could Eduardo Leones have dragged that treasure chest in here?"

"You're right!" said Grace. "It'd never fit through the crawl space."

"Exactly. I think the escape hatch is where the puzzle says the fire pit should be."

"Can you find it?" asked Grace.

"Yes. I just have to work the same sort of plane geometry to find another point not labeled on our map."

This time, it took Jake less than five minutes to complete the complex series of equations and find his vectors.

Thanks, Haazim, he thought. *Thanks, jelly beans!*

"We dig here!" he announced.

"Good job, genius!" said Kojo.

Out came the pickax and shovels again.

Please let me be right!

Up flew the gravel.

Three feet down, they hit wood.

"Yes!" shouted Kojo. "That sounds like a hatch if ever I heard one."

They dropped to their knees and cleared away more

stones to discover four one-foot-wide rough-hewn beams clamped together with thick metal bands along the edges.

"Looks like something the cabin boy could've salvaged from a shipwreck!" exclaimed Grace. "A wooden hatch from a deck. Maybe from the *Stinky Dog* after it sank."

"And," said Jake, "it's wide enough for the treasure chest."

"Grab hold of the handles, guys," said Kojo. "Maybe we can tilt it up on its far edge."

They leaned down and gripped the metal handholds on the near edge.

"On three," said Jake. "One, two, three!"

They heaved with all their might and, with a few more grunts, propped the ship's hatch open.

"Look," said Kojo. "There're ladder rungs down the side. It's like a maintenance hole leading down into the sewers."

A gust of air rushed up from the vertical tunnel and whacked them in their noses.

"Eww, what's that smell?" said Grace.

Jake sniffed the air the way a sophisticated connoisseur might.

"If I'm not mistaken, that's the familiar and fragrant scent of yesterday's french fries and deep-fried chicken nuggets."

"The cafeteria?" said Kojo.

Jake grinned. "Yep!"

"Then let's get out of here!" said Grace, scampering down the ladder first.

"I'm right behind you, baby," shouted Kojo. "I could really go for some french fries and chicken nuggets!"

69

The escape hatch led down to a very well-constructed stone corridor, like something you'd find in a medieval castle.

There were no electric lamps on the walls but plenty of torches for the taking. Three of them still had enough fuel to blaze through the darkness. And Kojo had remembered to pack waterproof matches. Because he was always prepared for anything.

"Man, how long did your ancient ancestor work on this project down here?" remarked Kojo, admiring the carefully crafted corridor of stone.

"Probably years," said Grace, holding up her torch. "But don't forget—they didn't have TV or video games back then. There wasn't much to do except build stuff."

"Up ahead!" said Jake. "See it? That's a shaft of light shining down through some kind of slats!"

Jake, Grace, and Kojo ran up the narrow cobblestone corridor to the dappled circle of light on the floor.

Where they all slipped and landed on their butts.

Their torches sizzled out in the pond of scum they'd just landed in because the floor beneath the overhead grate was slick with a pool of greasy water.

"That's the drain in the cafeteria floor!" said Grace, peering up twenty feet to a circular, slatted grate. "That's where Mr. Schroeder pushes all the slop when he mops."

"Gross, disgusting, and yet wonderful!" said Jake.

Iron climbing rungs were bolted into the stone sides of a circular silo leading up to the grate.

"Let's hope we can push that drain cover open," said Jake, leading the climb up the rusty ladder.

When he reached the top, it just took a good double-handed shove to send the grate wobbling across the cafeteria floor.

Jake helped Grace and then Kojo climb out of the hole.

"Now what?" said Kojo.

"First things first," said Grace. "We go rescue Uncle Charley."

"Then we come back and grab a snack!" added Kojo. "I'm still starving!"

The trio took off running down the empty hall.

They pushed open the vice principal's office door and found Mr. Lyons tied up on the floor.

Jake, who, probably thanks to one of the jelly beans, suddenly had an untapped mastery of sailing knots, quickly untied the vice principal's hands and feet while Grace carefully peeled the duct tape off his mouth.

"What? Where am I?" mumbled Mr. Lyons.

"Everything's okay, Uncle Charley," said Grace, filled with relief. "You're fine, we're fine."

"Who was that French guy who bopped me on the head?"

"Eriq LeVisqueux," said Kojo. "Known jewel thief and treasure hunter. But don't worry—the FBI and I are on his tail, sir."

"Did you find the treasure?"

"Yes, Uncle Charley," said Grace. "We did. It's magnificent. Unfortunately, some very bad people stole it from us."

"But don't worry about that, either, sir," said Jake. "We're going to get it back. Kojo?"

"Yeah?"

"Call our friends at the FBI."

"No problem. Special Agents Tillman and Andrus are still in the city, searching for Monsieur LeVisqueux."

"Have them meet us at the Imperial Marquis Hotel at nine."

"Why? LeVisqueux's not going to be there. He already has the treasure."

"Doesn't matter. Mrs. Malvolio will be there!"

Grace nodded. "She said so herself. She's probably planning a big scene for when we don't show up. She'll say and do something dramatic in front of Superintendent

Lopez and the press about how dangerous our building is, just to make sure Riverview Middle keeps its date with the bulldozers."

"Well, we can do something dramatic, too," said Jake. "After you call the FBI, Kojo, make sure your phone is good and charged. Can you edit together a shorter version of the video you shot down in the cave?"

"No problem. I'll cut a highlights reel. Us finding the treasure. Mrs. Malvolio, Heath Huxley, and LeVisqueux admitting we found it. The bad guys waving that sword and stealing our treasure—it'll be the best of the best. Like a trailer for a TV show!"

"Perfect," said Jake. "We nab Mrs. Malvolio, she'll give up the others."

"She'll fold faster than a cheap lawn chair, baby!" said Kojo.

Everybody stared at him.

"Sorry. That's just something we detectives say sometimes."

Jake turned to Grace's uncle. "Mr. Lyons?"

"Yeah?"

"Can you drive us to the hotel?

"Sure. No problemo."

"¡Fantástico!"

"And, Jake?"

"Yes, sir?"

"When this is all done, you should ask Grace to help you with your accent."

"Will do," Jake said. "We should probably leave here around eight-thirty. We don't want to show up at the hotel too early . . . or too late. We need to call our parental units. Let them know we're all okay—no matter what they hear from Mrs. Malvolio."

"Good idea," said Grace.

"But ask them to play along. Act surprised and shocked if Mrs. Malvolio tells them we're missing in a dangerous cavern underneath our even more dangerous school."

"My mom and dad are good actors," said Grace. "Mom fakes surprise and delight every time Dad gives her a bad Christmas present."

"My mom does that, too," said Kojo. "But seriously: Who gives someone a vacuum cleaner for Christmas?"

Jake laughed. It felt good to be with his friends. Hanging with these two? Probably the smartest thing he'd ever done.

"Okay, you guys," he said. "Let's charge our phones and make the calls. I also need to ask my mom for the password for the Apple TV system in the ballroom. Because that's where we're going to have the world premiere of Kojo's phone-movie masterpiece!"

70

Mr. Lyons drove Jake, Kojo, and Grace to the service entrance behind the downtown hotel.

"I wish I could go sit in the audience and watch the show," he said. "But that might give you guys away."

All parents had been contacted. They were relieved, on board, and ready to play their parts.

"The FBI is standing by, too," said Kojo. "Let me send you their number, Jake. This will put you right through to their earpieces when you need them."

"Perfect. Mom sent me the code for the Apple TV in the ballroom. That's how they're projecting the Quiz Bowl questions up to the two jumbo screens on either side of the stage. I'm sending it to you."

"Got it!"

With the help of his friend Tony, who was taking another break on the loading dock, Jake led his two teammates through the hotel's industrial-sized kitchen and into the greenroom.

The place where the whole jelly bean thing had started.

Jake turned up the volume for the video monitor mounted on the cinder-block wall. "We can watch everything from back here until it's time for us to make our entrance," he said. "There's no telling when our first round will be."

"Welcome one and all to the state finals of this year's Middle School Quiz Bowl competition," said the emcee, Haley James, the weather reporter from the biggest TV station in the state. "Let's get this tournament started. Each team will field ten questions. The top scoring teams in the preliminary rounds will move up to the next bracket. We'll keep eliminating teams until the top two face off for the title of state champion!"

The audience applauded.

"All right, let's welcome our first contestants: Riverview Middle School and their upstate rivals Farragut Middle School."

"What?" said Kojo. "We're up first?"

"Excuse me!" cried Mrs. Malvolio, bustling through the packed ballroom, working her way toward the stage. "Excuse me! Principal of Riverview. Coming through. I have horrible news!"

"Let's go, you guys," said Jake. "We're on."

He trotted out of the greenroom and weaved his way

across the kitchen to the ballroom stage entrance. Kojo and Grace were trotting right behind him.

They could hear the crowd murmuring as Mrs. Malvolio pushed her way to the podium.

"I'm Patricia Malvolio," she said. "As principal of Riverview Middle School, it is my sad duty to report that I have absolutely no idea where our team might be. I think the pressure was too much. They caved."

She giggled slightly, enjoying her own inside joke.

The crowd moaned.

"I know," said Mrs. Malvolio. "I too am severely disappointed in them."

Jake speed-dialed the FBI agents and whispered, "Go!" just as the Riverview team stepped onstage.

A spotlight hit the three students.

People gasped.

Mrs. Malvolio gasped the loudest.

"I knew they'd never give up!" shouted Mr. Keeney, seated in the front row.

"Way to go, team!" cheered Noah "No Neck" Nelson.

Jake's, Grace's, and Kojo's clothes were dirty and dusty—not to mention slightly torn. Their faces and hair were a mess. Their butts were soggy. They didn't care.

"We didn't cave, you guys," Jake said into the nearest microphone. "Riverview Pirates never give up. But we did spend some time in a cave last night. Can we dim the houselights, please? Hit it, Kojo."

Kojo tapped a button on his phone.

The two giant video monitors on either side of the stage were instantly filled with a grainy, sixty-second movie about everything that happened in the cavern. Grace, Kojo, and Jake digging up the buried treasure. Celebrating. Tossing gold coins up into the air. (That earned a few laughs.) Mrs. Malvolio bursting into the room. LeVisqueux waving his sword, admitting what they were doing.

"Zees is my favorite way to hunt for zee treasure," everyone heard LeVisqueux say. "Let some other fool find eet, and zen steal eet out from under zem."

"Boo!" shouted Noah Nelson from the audience. "That dude's the bad guy."

The next shot showed the famous real estate tycoon Heath Huxley chuckling, "Thanks for doing our digging, kids."

Noah threw his arms up over his head. "Another bad guy!" The whole crowd started booing.

The screen cut to Mrs. Malvolio joking, "I'll make sure you all get extra credit for it."

Now the crowd was hissing on top of the boos.

"We found the treasure," proclaimed Grace on the screen. "Therefore, it's ours."

The crowd rose to its feet and cheered.

The closing line went to Mr. Huxley: "Not if we steal it from you first!"

The cheers became a horrified grumble.

"Lights, please," said Jake.

Mrs. Malvolio was still onstage. She was smiling, batting her eyes, and fidgeting with her clunky necklace. But she wasn't budging. Because she was flanked by the two FBI agents, Tillman and Andrus.

The school superintendent, Dr. Lopez, was in the first row, steaming.

"I know where you can find Uncle Heath!" blurted Mrs. Malvolio. "And the treasure. And Eriq LeVisqueux. I'm ready to make a deal!"

"Let's talk about it outside," said Special Agent Tillman as she escorted the principal off the stage.

"Good luck in the Quiz Bowl, kids!" Mrs. Malvolio shouted, giving Jake, Grace, and Kojo another one of her lipstick-crackling smiles. "I love children. And being a principal. I don't know what I was doing down in that cave. It was stress. Being the principal of a middle school is a very stressful job. That's why we had a sword. It was my emotional support sword. Superintendent Lopez? Are you here, Rosalia? I think I need a vacation."

Superintendent Lopez had made her way onto the stage.

"Oh, you're going to get one, Patricia," said the superintendent. "A nice, long vacation. Probably five to ten years."

"Woo-hoo!" shouted Grace, Jake, and Kojo as the audience applauded wildly.

"And tell your uncle," Superintendent Lopez added,

"we're not tearing down Riverview Middle School. Not now, not ever. How could we, when it produces geniuses such as Kojo Shelton, Grace Garcia, and, of course, Jake McQuade!"

The TV news crews followed the FBI agents and the disgraced principal out of the ballroom.

"Maybe we should all take a short break before we begin," said the emcee.

The ballroom burst into another standing ovation.

Not because of the break.

They were cheering for Grace, Kojo, and Jake.

EPILOGUE

Riverview Middle School went on to win the State Quiz Bowl competition.

Grace, Kojo, and Jake took turns answering questions. They didn't miss a single one.

With invaluable assistance from Mrs. Malvolio, who, as Kojo predicted, sang like a bird and folded like a cheap suitcase (two more of his favorite detective clichés), the FBI quickly apprehended and arrested both Heath Huxley and Eriq LeVisqueux.

A judge ruled that Grace Garcia, because she was related to Eduardo Leones and had led the expedition to dig up the cabin boy's treasure, was entitled to everything buried underneath the school. After giving 10 percent to Jake and Kojo, Grace gave half of her share to her uncle (who didn't buy an island in the Caribbean—just new basketball uniforms for his team).

But even after she had given away 55 percent of her wealth, Grace was still the richest twelve-year-old in the world. She immediately set up a trust fund for the "perpetual betterment of Riverview Middle School and all struggling public education facilities in the city."

Kojo donated most of his treasure money to the same fund. But he kept enough to buy a complete, professional-grade forensics investigation kit.

Jake used the bulk of his earnings to finance Haazim Farooqi's room, board, and tuition for the biomedical engineering PhD program at New Jersey's Rutgers University.

"Thank you, Subject One," Mr. Farooqi told him. "They're giving me my own lab. Meanwhile, don't tell them, but I'm purchasing mass quantities of research supplies: sugar, gelatin, cornstarch and . . . jelly bean molds!"

Mr. Charley Lyons, the (now) extremely wealthy vice principal, was promoted to principal of Riverview. Mr. Keeney became his new second-in-command.

Jake's mom and little sister had never been prouder of him.

Not because he'd won the State Quiz Bowl competition. Because he'd given away his share of the treasure.

"With great power comes great responsibility," he reminded them.

They laughed. And asked him to quit saying that.

* * *

Three weeks later, things had started to settle down.

No one was asking for autographs anymore, and Jake was back to his regular life—only with really good grades, some amazing Spanish dinners, and time spent "sending the elevator back down"—tutoring kids (including Emma) who needed a little help with their homework.

One day Jake was bopping down the freshly painted halls of Riverview Middle School, admiring the rows of shiny new lockers. He knocked knuckles with his pals and headed to homeroom. He had another interesting math puzzle to challenge Mr. Keeney with.

Suddenly, Principal Lyons stepped out of his office.

"Jake?" he said, sounding super serious.

"Yes, sir? Is everything okay?"

"Can you come with me? There are some folks who need to speak to you. They say it's urgent."

Jake followed the principal into the office and his small conference room.

General Joe Coleman, the one Jake had worked with at the Pentagon, was waiting with his hands clasped firmly behind his back. Two military personnel with almost as many ribbons on their chests were with him.

In the distance, Jake could hear the familiar *whump-whump-whump* of a helicopter's whirring rotors.

Jake sighed. *Guess I won't be making paella tonight.*

"Mr. McQuade?" barked General Coleman.

"Yes, sir?"

"We have another situation. And it's a bad one. Your country needs you, son. Now!"

Jake nodded.

With great power came great responsibility.

He was off on his next mission.

Are YOU as Smart as the Smartest Kid in the Universe?

Here are a few more puzzles from Jake's IQ test!

Can you keep up with Jake? Solve these puzzles and show the smartest kid in the universe just how smart *you* are! Find out if you're correct at ChrisGrabenstein.com.

SQUARE PUZZLES

Slice this picture into two identical, symmetrical parts.

Slice this picture into four identical parts.

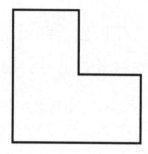

How many squares are in this diagram?

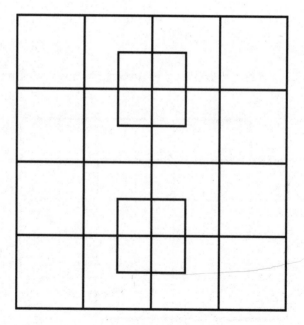

Bowls, I'm Baffled!

You have a 10-liter bowl, a 6-liter bowl, and unlimited access to water. How do you measure exactly 8 liters?

Marvelous Marbles

You have nine marbles that are similar in size. Eight of them weigh the same, but the ninth one is a bit heavier. If you could use a two-pan balance scale *only twice*, how would you identify the heavy marble?

Clear Dots, Black Dots, No Dots!

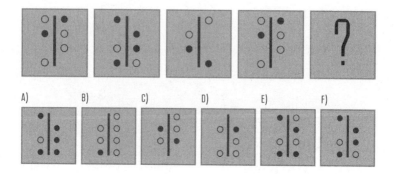

A)   B)   C)   D)   E)   F)

Can you figure out which image completes the following
sequence? Extra points if you can explain why!

[Dis]Organize These Pencils

You have six pencils. Can you arrange them in such
a way that each pencil is touching all five of the others?
Grab a piece of paper and draw your response.

READY FOR RIDDLES?

What gets wetter the more it dries?

What can you catch but not throw?

No sooner spoken than broken. What is it?

What goes up and down the stairs without moving?

I am weightless, but you can see me. Put me in a
bucket, and I'll make it lighter. What am I?

I'm where yesterday follows today, and tomorrow's in
between. What am I?

I fly, but I have no wings. I cry, but I have no eyes.
Darkness follows me. What am I?

Don't miss Book 2

THE SMARTEST KID IN THE UNIVERSE

GENIUS CAMP

coming in 2021!

"Chris Grabenstein just might be the smartest writer for kids in the universe. No kid, and no adult, will be able to resist *The Smartest Kid in the Universe*."
— JAMES PATTERSON

"Clever, fast-paced, and incredibly funny— Chris Grabenstein has done it again."
— STUART GIBBS, *NEW YORK TIMES* BESTSELLING AUTHOR OF THE SPY SCHOOL SERIES

Thank You to . . .

My brilliant wife (and coauthor of *Shine!*), J.J. The smartest thing I ever did was marry her.

My longtime Random House editor, Shana Corey. She might just be the smartest editor in the universe. Extra thanks for helping me create the first chapter of a whole new series.

Polo Orozco, for his editorial assistance (and congratulations on your promotion).

My even longer-time literary agent and a smartly dressed man-about-town, Eric Myers.

The gifted and talented math wizards who helped me with the treasure map: Erin Allen, Kimberlie Grabenstein, and Mike Wilson.

Nicholas Negroponte, founder of the MIT Media Laboratory, whose TED Talk "A Thirty-Year History of the Future" served as the inspiration for *The Smartest Kid in the Universe*.

Many thanks for the brilliant authenticity reads and translation assistance from Polo Orozco, Mariam Quraishi, Dani Valladares, and Brittany N. Williams.

The very smart cover was created by Antoine Losty.

Thanks to him and Michelle Cunningham, Katrina Damkoehler, Stephanie Moss, Trish Parcell, Martha Rago, April Ward, and everybody in the Random House Children's Books art department.

An author is just one part of the team that makes a book. Special thanks to all the supersmart folks at Random House:

John Adamo, Kerri Benvenuto, Julianne Conlon, Janet Foley, Judith Haut, Kate Keating, Jules Kelly, Gillian Levinson, Mallory Loehr, Barbara Marcus, Kelly McGauley, Michelle Nagler, and Janine Perez.

Copyediting: Barbara Bakowski, Alison Kolani, and Christine Ma.

Production: Shameiza Ally and Tim Terhune.

Publicity: Dominique Cimina, Lili Feinberg, and Noreen Herits.

School and Library Marketing: Emily DuVal, Shaughnessy Miller, Emily Petrick, Kristin Schulz, Erica Stone, and Adrienne Waintraub.

Sales (the geniuses who get the right books into the right kids' hands): Suzanne Archer, Amanda Auch, Emily Bruce, Gretchen Chapman, Brenda Conway, Dandy Conway, Whitney Conyers, Stephanie Davey, Jenelle Davis, Nic DuFort, Cletus Durkin, Felicia Frazier, Stella Galatis, Alex Gottlieb, Becky Green, Susan Hecht, Christina Jeffries, Kimberly Langus, Katie Lenox, Ruth Liebmann, Lauren Mackey, Cindy Mapp, Dennis McLaughlin, Deanna Meyerhoff, Carol Monteiro, Tim Mooney, Stacey

Pyle, Michele Sadler, Mark Santella, William Steedman, Ceara Steffan, Kate Sullivan, and Richard Vallejo.

And finally, thanks to all the teachers and librarians who work tirelessly to prepare students for jobs that may not even exist yet but will definitely require a ton of smarts.

CHRIS GRABENSTEIN

is the #1 *New York Times* bestselling author of the hilarious and critically acclaimed Mr. Lemoncello's Library and Welcome to Wonderland series, *The Island of Dr. Libris, Shine!* (coauthored with J.J. Grabenstein), and many other books, as well as the coauthor of numerous page-turners with James Patterson, including *Katt vs. Dogg* and the Treasure Hunters and Max Einstein series. Chris loves jelly beans and has always secretly suspected he might be a genius (but no one seems to agree with him). Chris lives in New York City with his wife, J.J. Visit ChrisGrabenstein.com for trailers, fun facts, and more.

🐦 @cgrabenstein
📘 cgrabber1955
📷 chris.grabenstein